A Feast for the Eyes

Leaning back against the willow tree, sipping wine, Sarah thought, *I could remain here forever.* Then she realized something with a jolt.

Paul felt her eyes on him and looked up, seeing the change in her. "What is it?"

"I—I was wondering why I've heard nothing from my father. I fear he no longer wants me."

Paul sat up. "That's nonsense, Sarah. Of course he wants you. Anyway"—he smiled—"there's always a place for you at Mannerby."

She returned the smile. "That would lack propriety, Paul."

He leaned back again. "I've already thought of that—and my aunt Mathilda in London will make an excellent chaperone for you."

Later, he paused as he put the glasses back into the hamper, watching her as she gathered her irises. Perhaps it was just as well.that Aunt Mathilda was coming, he thought, for Sarah was tantalizingly lovely and he found himself enjoying her company far too much. . . .

SIGNET

REGENCY ROMANCE
COMING IN JULY 2005

A Splendid Indiscretion and
The Grand Passion
by Elizabeth Mansfield
Two novels from "one of the best-loved authors of
Regency romance" (*Romance Reader*) together for the
first time in one volume.

0-451-21624-5

Her Perfect Earl
by Bethany Brooks
Esmerelda Fortune would never have accepted the
position of governess to the Earl of Ashforth's infa-
mous brood of five children if it weren't for Corina, an
ancient manuscript in the widower's possession. But
soon she will have new reasons for wanting to stay in
his employ.

0-451-21599-0

Lady Silence
by Blair Bancroft
Damon Farr, a war-weary cavalry colonel in search of
peace and quiet, acquires a good deal more when he
employs as his secretary Katy Snow, the mute house-
maid his family took in off the streets years earlier.

0-451-21586-9

The Whispering Rocks

Sandra Heath

Previously published as
Mannerby's Lady

A SIGNET BOOK

SIGNET
Published by New American Library, a division of
Penguin Group (USA) Inc., 375 Hudson Street,
New York, New York 10014, USA
Penguin Group (Canada), 10 Alcorn Avenue, Toronto,
Ontario M4V 3B2, Canada (a division of Pearson Penguin Canada Inc.)
Penguin Books Ltd., 80 Strand, London WC2R 0RL, England
Penguin Ireland, 25 St. Stephen's Green, Dublin 2,
Ireland (a division of Penguin Books Ltd.)
Penguin Group (Australia), 250 Camberwell Road, Camberwell, Victoria 3124,
Australia (a division of Pearson Australia Group Pty. Ltd.)
Penguin Books India Pvt. Ltd., 11 Community Centre, Panchsheel Park,
New Delhi - 110 017, India
Penguin Group (NZ), cnr Airborne and Rosedale Roads, Albany,
Auckland 1310, New Zealand (a division of Pearson New Zealand Ltd.)
Penguin Books (South Africa) (Pty.) Ltd., 24 Sturdee Avenue,
Rosebank, Johannesburg 2196, South Africa

Penguin Books Ltd., Registered Offices:
80 Strand, London WC2R 0RL, England

Published by Signet, an imprint of New American Library, a division of Penguin Group (USA) Inc. Previously published as *Mannerby's Lady*.

First Signet Printing, June 2005
10 9 8 7 6 5 4 3 2 1

Author's Note

The Whispering Rocks is a rewritten, much more mysterious version of *Mannerby's Lady*. It is still a Regency, but has become a darker tale of witchcraft and jealousy, of misplaced trust and eventual true love. If you enjoy a Gothic romance, then please read on. . . .

Chapter One

$\mathcal{A}$s the hunt streamed down the track from Rook House and into the woods which straddled the sloping parkland, Jack Holland reined in, maneuvering his nervous bay carefully into the trees and then turning to stare back along the way. The crisp January air echoed with the yelping of the hounds and with the wavering sound of the hunting horns as Sir Peter Stratford's guests set off for the first chase of the new year. No one noticed that Jack had left them, and he paid scant attention to the change of note as the hounds picked up a scent. He was more concerned with the strange behavior of his host's charming daughter, the beautiful Sarah Jane.

She had dropped back from the hunt only a short while before, drawing up her shambling, lop-eared mare with some difficulty because she was so unused to riding sidesaddle, and now she was staring down a path which wound away through the woods toward a small valley. Indecision clouded her pretty face and she bit her lip, leaning forward to pat the lowered neck of her mount. Her thick black hair was piled into Grecian curls on the top of which rested a beaver hat, and the rich crimson velvet of her riding habit accentuated the full curves of her body. Jack allowed his gaze to wander appreciatively over her. Heaven alone knew how a boor like Stratford had managed to sire such a beauty. One could not guess by looking at her that she was illegitimate and had until recently known only poverty. She looked every inch the lady; except perhaps— He smiled a little as he saw how uncomfortable she was on the sidesaddle and how she flinched when her tightly-laced stays dug into her. He raised an eyebrow as he saw how expertly she controlled the mare; perhaps there was more to her than first met the eye. She was obviously an accomplished horsewoman, and suddenly the strange choice of so docile a mount seemed not to proclaim her a timid rider but rather to tell of her wiliness—it was better to be laughed at for riding such a creature than to be ridiculed for falling off a more spirited mount. She shifted awkwardly on the sidesaddle again, glancing after the hunt and then back toward the pathway.

Jack dismounted, for the bay was restless at being kept so quiet. He went to its head and gently rubbed its soft muzzle, his attention still on the girl. What could she be up to? Why did she hover there? Another movement caught his eye as a small red animal slid across the clearing behind him, its brush dragging through the crisp dead leaves. He smiled as the fox made good its escape.

Flicking an imaginary speck of dust from his impeccable dark blue sleeve, he leaned against the trunk of a tree, still staring at Sarah. Everything about the faultless cut of his clothes bore the stamp of Weston of Old Bond Street. The collar of his snow-white shirt rose on either side of his thin, good-looking face, curving outward like wings, and at his throat blossomed a cravat of immense proportion which somehow contrived to look most excellent. He was a nonpareil, a man of great influence at the court of his close friend the Prince Regent; and the cynical eyebrows of the *beau monde* would indeed have been raised had they seen him skulking so secretively in the trees spying on Sir Peter Stratford's intriguing daughter.

Unaware that she was being so closely scrutinized, Sarah took the note out of her reticule and read it yet again, although she knew its contents by heart. A sigh escaped her. What should she do? She knew what she *wanted* to do, but she knew also in her heart what she *ought* to do. Common sense bade her ignore the note and hurry after the hunt, but her own sense of unhappiness and insecurity, her desperate need of a friend prodded her to keep the tryst with Ralph Jameson on the bridge in the woods. Firmly she gathered the reins and urged the mare down the overgrown pathway, and the note fluttered unnoticed to the ground.

Slowly Jack led his horse out of the trees and bent to retrieve the scrap of paper. His gray eyes narrowed as he read. Thoughtfully he pulled his top hat down firmly on his curling copper hair, remounted, and followed Sarah.

The slow clip-clop of the mare's hooves sounded loud beneath the overhanging branches. The night's frost was now melting fast and everything was damp and cold. The wind whispered between the tall trunks with a chill clamminess and Sarah was now almost glad of the stays which so restricted her movements but served to keep her warm. Dark green ivy leaves glistened and rustled, and scarlet holly berries made bright splashes of color in the grayness of the winter woodland. In the distance she heard the hunt and glanced around as if expecting to be followed, but there was no one there. Had she been missed? No, she doubted it, for the actions of Stratford's illegitimate daughter would pale to insignificance beside the thrill of a good hunt.

The first tinkling sound of the stream caught her ear as it gurgled and splashed along the floor of the valley. A blackbird was startled and its excited calls of alarm swung round and round the silently dripping trees. She held her breath; it was only a bird—

Away to her right Jack's bay stallion moved quietly through the woods, but she heard and saw nothing as she rode on. Slumbering willows draped their branches over the stream and she saw the tight buds of pussy willow along the thick margin of bushes at the water's edge. A water rat plopped heavily into the stream and vanished from sight. Surely the bridge was somewhere near now? Would he be there?

As the thought entered her head she heard a horse whinnying gently in greeting. And then she saw Ralph. The bridge was there, hidden by a confusion of catkins and alders, and leaning against the rustic wooden parapet was a young man of slender build, dressed in an oatmeal coat. A riding crop swung idly to and fro in his gloved hands and he gazed thoughtfully at the rushing stream. His dark brown hair was arranged neatly in rows of tight curls and an eyeglass dangled round his neck on a golden chain. As she approached he heard and glanced up. Even from that distance she could see the brilliance of his china blue eyes—and the black patch which adorned the corner of his mouth. He smiled and came along the bridge to meet her.

Shyness stole over her then, for she knew that her actions in coming here were questionable and that she hardly knew him; but he did not know about her forthcoming marriage or how desperately unhappy she was. He was her only friend, and she felt so very lonely. As she saw the warmth in his eyes she was glad she had come. He stretched up and lifted her from the saddle, his hands strong around her waist. How she longed to be enclosed in his arms, safe and protected. She walked quickly on to the bridge, blushing at her own forward thoughts.

She was flustered. "I know that I shouldn't have come—"

"I'm glad that you did, although it's surely more than I had any right to hope." The practiced ease with which he spoke showed, but she wanted only to cling to each word. In a month at Rook House only Ralph had been kind. Only Ralph. She smiled at him with more warmth than was advisable.

He came nearer, his hand resting against her waist as she leaned over the bridge. "My poor little country mouse, are you unhappy?" he asked gently. He was perfumed and his cheeks were slightly rouged, but she did not care; if such was the fashion among the dandies, who was she to comment?

She nodded miserably in answer to his question. How foolish and vain it had been to have so looked forward to the new year of 1815. She had thought that a new period in her life was to begin, a period of luxury and happiness—but instead she was to marry her cousin Edward who hated her and would do all he could to make her life as miserable as it had been before her arrival at Rook House. Ralph did not know yet. "Oh, Ralph, everything has gone so sour since last I saw you. I thought when my father came to Longwicke and brought me back to Rook House that he—well, that he had come out of parental love. But he hadn't. He came for me because my cousin Edward had been seriously courting some girl my father doesn't approve of. I'm here solely as a wife for Edward. He must marry me or lose the Stratford inheritance."

Her back was toward Ralph; otherwise she would have seen the change which came over his face. So, she was marked for Edward, was she? His handsome face showed his anger. His plans were thwarted. He had played his cards so well, too, or so he thought, for she would have fallen into his hands like a ripe plum, and with her eventually would have come old Stratford's fortune. But if her father's plan was not to disinherit Edward, merely to foil him, then of what use was his pursuit of the delightful Sarah? His hand lingered against her waist but it was no longer relaxed and confident. His thoughts were in turmoil, his rage overwhelming, and directed now against the girl who thought herself so safe with him.

She turned to look at him suddenly. "That's why I'm so unhappy, Ralph. I—" Her voice broke off, dying instantly as she saw the twisting muscles of his face. Alarmed she tried to step away, but his fingers tightened on her waist, pinching cruelly.

"You've wasted my time, Miss Stratford. You've sorely wasted my time!" But still, he thought grudgingly, she was one of the most beautiful and desirable women he had ever seen. His tongue passed over his dry lips as he felt her begin to struggle. He had a mind to taste the charms which were destined for the oafish Edward. Roughly he dragged her into his arms and forced his parted lips down upon her mouth.

Chapter Two

High on the slope beyond the bridge Jack Holland reined in and put his hand to his eyes to shield them from a shaft of sunlight which pierced the web of trees. He stared down the hillside toward the pair on the bridge. Slowly he took off his top hat and ran his fingers through his burnished hair, his fingers pausing in their movement as the frightened struggles of the girl became more obvious. Perhaps Stratford's daughter was not playing the coquette with Jameson after all. Jack replaced his top hat and reached inside his dark blue coat.

Terror infused Sarah's struggles now and she beat her fists against Ralph helplessly. Tears almost blinded her and she could not speak, for her voice seemed paralyzed. Her efforts to escape seemed only to spur him on still more.

A shot rang out and a bullet whined against the parapet, striking splinters in all directions. Ralph released her instantly, cursing and staring up toward the solitary figure on the bay. "Holland! I recognize that red-headed devil even from this distance!"

But he spoke to the empty air for she had seized her chance and was running toward her mount, which seemed completely unaffected by the pistol shot. But Ralph's stallion was gone, its frightened hooves drumming on the mossy ground, its ears flat and its tail flying. It is no easy matter to run for your life on soft ground wearing riding boots, but somehow Ralph accomplished the impossible as he saw Jack begin to descend the slope.

Sarah's shoes sank into the soft, sucking mud at the water's edge where the placid mare drank with irritating calm. The mud was slippery and she lost her foothold. With a cry she toppled over into the ice-cold water. The pins which held her hair were dislodged and the black tresses tumbled down over her face. Her silly hat with its ostrich feathers was snatched away and bobbed like a tiny boat upon the stream, vanishing beneath the span of the bridge. Her dismay was complete and she sat in the water, weeping bitterly.

Jack's horse carried him swiftly to the stream and he was soon reaching out to help her, but she sat there crying. He had no intention of stepping into the water in his excellent boots, and sighed as he wondered how to dispel her tears.

"Miss Stratford, do you intend to remain there all day?" He spoke to no avail, for she continued to sit looking very foolish but unable to help herself.

His sharp gray eyes caught a new movement high on the hill, a figure in a bright purple riding habit and wearing a hat of the same vivid color. Lady Hermione Stratford! What was Edward's fearsome mother doing here? No doubt looking for the missing heiress, as he himself had been. His thin lips curved into a cold smile and he looked back at Sarah. "Madam, if you wish to be discovered thus by Lady Hermione, then by all means do so, but I'd advise you to come out now and save appearances all you can."

His bantering tone penetrated at last. She struggled to her feet, her heart thundering with still more dismay, and her skirts clinging to every curve of her body. Jack stared at her. She thought nothing of his gaze; she could think only of the imminence of Lady Hermione, the one person who had done more than anyone else to make her life at Rook House a misery. She reached out to take Jack's hand, her teeth chattering and her sobs gradually subsiding.

He removed his coat and placed it around her shivering shoulders, glancing up the hillside to see that Hermione's mount was coming down toward the bridge. Sarah's eyes bore a haunted look as she saw the splash of purple moving relentlessly nearer. This was the end of her then. She would have to return to Longwicke—to the advances of Squire Eldon, who had made no secret of his intentions. There was nowhere else in the world for her to go except whence she had come. She swallowed. The tale of today's exploits would be the delighted talk of the drawing room this afternoon, and would be whispered about over dinner. She had by her actions made her father look foolish, a laughingstock, and had played straight into the hands of Lady Hermione and cousin Edward. Edward would make his protests loudly, and with justification, and her father would almost certainly be forced to pay attention. Unexpectedly she smiled, wiping her face with a muddy hand which left a streak across her white cheek. Well, she certainly was a poor judge of character, for she could hardly have been more wrong about Ralph Jameson.

Lady Hermione drew her mount to a standstill, her little eyes fixed on Sarah's odd appearance. This was all very interesting. How wise she had been to come looking for Stratford's brat. And here she was—with Jack Holland, of all men! What had been going on? She noticed the resignation on Sarah's face, making her look like a whipped dog. It seemed too good to be true. Hermione leaned forward. "Whatever has happened, Mr. Holland?"

"Miss Stratford had rather a nasty fall from her horse. It was fortunate that I saw her and hurried to help."

Sarah blinked, her lips parting. He was not going to tell anything! Her dull eyes brightened and hope struggled back into her. She loathed the prospect of marriage with her cousin Edward, but she was frightened by the thought of returning to her previous life. She wished desperately that she had never come to meet Ralph, and now it seemed that Mr. Holland was

giving her a second chance. Jack felt her back
straighten a little and saw her raise her head. A little
of her former self reemerged and he liked what he
saw.

Hermione, meanwhile, was gaping at the gray mare.
A fall? From *that?* One might as well tumble off a
sofa! She sniffed, her mouth sliding sideways disbelievingly. There must be more to it.

Jack maneuvered Sarah toward the mare. "Pray
continue with your plans, Lady Hermione. I'll accompany Miss Stratford back to the house." He spoke
politely, but Hermione realized she was being dismissed. Her eyes hardened. She had never liked him,
for she had never been able to get the better of him.
He rode so high in the land, had so much influence
at court and was so close to the Regent. He was accepted by all the best clubs and his yellow phaeton
was one of the finest sights in Hyde Park. He was
everywhere, did everything, and knew everyone who
was anyone. He had vanquished Edward at the gaming
tables, and had beaten him too in a horse race of some
importance the previous season—and what was more
he chose to remind everyone of the fact by bringing
that cursed bay stallion with him to Rook House. And
why, after all this time, had he suddenly decided to
accept an invitation here? Bitterly, Hermione thought
of her brother-in-law's delight at discovering that the
great Jack Holland was at long last honoring Rook
House with his presence. She cursed the all-consuming
ambition of Stratford's to be one of the inner circle
of gentlemen surrounding the Prince Regent. Stratford
was one of the richest men in England, so why had
there to be a need to bother with people like Holland?
Hermione felt as if her mouth was filled with vinegar
as she stared at Jack. Only his influence at court gave
him any consequence, she thought furiously, for he
was a man of little true breeding. Her blue blood was
all she had left to flaunt before him, and she did so,
often. But now she decided prudently to leave, because for her purposes it was better that Sarah should

return to the house with Holland, alone, *and* in such a state of disarray!

Hermione turned her horse and smiled unpleasantly; very well, she would go back to join the hunt—and spread the tale of what she had come upon in the woods. The smile became feline. Aye, she would spread the scandal thickly, with perhaps the merest soupçon of a raised eyebrow. All was fair in love and war, and Hermione considered herself most definitely at war with Sarah—and with Jack Holland.

Jack recognized the expression on her face. Ah well, there was little he could do to prevent what she now intended, but he would do all in his power to keep the real truth from the sour old harridan and her avaricious son. He lifted Sarah on to the broad back of her mare and then mounted himself, leading both horses slowly away from the bridge.

Hermione watched until they were out of sight before riding back to join her companions who still hunted noisily over the surrounding countryside. In her mind she turned over what she had seen, drawing from it every tiny vestige of scandal, and choosing carefully what she would say. She must take care with this, for Stratford was perverse enough to take his daughter's side, especially if Holland's name was mentioned. And that would never do. Deep in her schemings, Hermione rode back up the slope.

For a long while Sarah did not speak as she looked ahead at Jack's straight back. She owed him much, for he had not only saved her from Ralph's advances, but also from Lady Hermione's spite. Why had he bothered with her? He had hardly spoken to her until this day.

They reached the edge of the woods and were looking up toward Rook House with its mellow stone walls and square towers. The reeds of the moat swayed, although the water itself was invisible from where they were. The rooks which gave the house its name wheeled above the roofs, excited by the hunt.

"Mr. Holland." Her voice was husky with the cold so she cleared her throat and repeated, "Mr. Holland."

He turned to look at her. Would nothing dim her beauty? Even the fall into the stream had done little to spoil her loveliness. Her hazel eyes were large as she spoke again. "Mr. Holland, I don't know how to thank you."

"Sarah, I think I'd so much prefer to hear my first name upon your lips. 'Mr. Holland' sounds so stiff and formal. Please call me Jack."

Wariness crept into her eyes. After her experience with Ralph she trusted no one.

He smiled then. "Don't look like that, for I mean you no harm. It's just that I abhor being called 'Mr. Holland' by one whom I admire and like."

"Until this moment you have shown no inclination to either liking or admiring me, Mr. Holland. I'm deeply in your debt and the feeling is very uncomfortable." There was an edge to her voice.

"That's the spirit, Sarah. Trust no one in this life and you'll do well enough." His voice bore a wealth of feeling.

She shivered, her teeth beginning to chatter again. He kicked his heel and the horses moved off toward the house.

Chapter Three

Sarah's maid Betty halted in horror when she saw her mistress's bedraggled appearance.

Like a little sparrow she hurried forward. "Oh, miss!" in her London accent was more pronounced than usual as she unhooked and unbuttoned the riding habit which was so utterly spoiled. "Whatever's 'appened to you?" She fussed around busily, her little face bothered. She was only Sarah's age but she bustled around her as if she was a generation older. Even as a mere maid she knew more of the ways of the gentry than did Sarah, and so she felt that she must guide and protect her all she could.

"I met with an accident, Betty. Mr. Holland rescued me and brought me back safely."

The deft fingers paused ominously. "An accident, miss? Mr. 'Olland?"

Sarah bit her lip. Perhaps it was best to continue the story invented by Mr. Holland for Lady Hermione's benefit, but, oh, how good it would be to unburden herself to Betty, whom she liked. "Yes, my horse threw me and I fell into a stream. Then I had to wade through mud to get out." Well, at least it was *half* the truth!

Betty carefully hung the riding habit on a hanger, tutting as she looked at it. Perhaps it could be saved, if care was taken—she would see to it personally. She took her mistress's turquoise robe and held it before the fire to warm, glancing now and then at the shivering figure in her white stays and undergarments.

Feeling the constant glances, Sarah raised her eyes. "What is it, Betty? What's bothering you?"

The maid stood there awkwardly. "P'raps it's not my place to say, miss, but—"

"But what?"

"Well, it's Mr. 'Olland being the one to bring you back."

"It's as well for me that he was there." Oh, how true *that* was!

"Yes, miss." There was a noticeable lack of conviction in the maid's voice.

"What is it about him in particular then? He was the perfect gentleman."

" 'E's got a *name,* miss, an awful name." Betty's eyes rolled dramatically.

"That hardly surprises me. He's handsome, wealthy, and unmarried. He's bound to possess a reputation for something or other." Sarah smiled. "Most probably for women!"

Betty's smile was weak. "That's as may be, miss, but 'e's s'posed to be more *evil* than that."

"Evil?"

"Yes, miss. Things've 'appened—all sorts of goings-on. There was 'is wife—"

"He's married?" Sarah was startled by this revelation.

" 'E *was,* miss, but she's dead now, poor soul. And it's the *way* she died! Being left alone in that great big 'ouse for month after month, and 'er so ill. It weren't right. An' all the time 'e kept 'is mistress in a fine 'ouse in London. Shameful it was, right enough." Betty finished her speech with flourish.

Sarah felt somehow that she should defend him. "If his wife was ill then surely she *had* to remain behind, and, anyway, most men keep mistresses, do they not?"

"She was ill, nigh to death itself, an' still 'e stayed away from 'er. It was so cruel, an' 'er so sweet a lady."

Sarah slipped her arms into the warm robe. It was

not pleasant to hear such tales of Mr. Holland, for he did not seem a cruel, heartless man and, besides, she had much to thank him for. "Did you know his wife then?"

"Oh no, miss, my cousin Liza was in service there. *She* told me all about it when she came 'ere—a great favorite with Sir Peter is my Liza. Anyway, when I saw Mr. 'Olland's name on the guest list I was proper put out. I made up my mind to stay right out of 'is way; it's not good even to look at anyone as bad as 'e is." Superstition oozed from Betty, for she seemed to think that by staying out of his way she broke some enchantment he had cast over her.

"You sound like a page from the very latest romantic novel, Betty. Tell me, your cousin Liza, is she—I mean—" Sarah's voice trailed away on an embarrassed note and she wished that she had not begun the question. Liza was the name of her father's poor, disregarded mistress, but how could she ask Betty if her cousin was the same Liza?

Betty colored a little. "Yes, miss. Liza's Sir Peter's mistress. Proper furious my mother would be if she knew, 'cause she's always looked after 'er since 'er own mother died. Still, she's got pretty clothes now, and lots of other things she wouldn't 'ave as a lady's maid, so I 'spect she thinks it's worth it."

"My father doesn't exactly maintain her lavishly, does he?"

"Well, she don't ask for anything and so 'e don't bother. Why should 'e if she's fool enough— Begging your pardon, miss." Betty feared that she had gone too far.

"I don't mind, Betty." It was true. Any warm feelings she may have had for her father had vanished the day he told her the truth about his entry into her life, that he needed her only to bring Edward to his senses.

"Liza 'ad to go to the inquest." Betty was impressed and spoke almost reverently.

"Inquest?"

"Yes, miss, the one they 'ad 'cause of the way Mrs.

'Olland died. They said she'd been *poisoned!*" This was obviously the maid's trump card.

Sarah tried not to show how much this shocked her. She sat down before her dressing table. "Then the blame can hardly be placed at Mr. Holland's feet, can it? You said yourself that he wouldn't go near his wife."

"That's what 'e wanted them all to think, miss, but 'e got someone else to do 'is dirty work. That's what they say anyway."

"Oh, that's enough, Betty. After all he's my father's guest and I have no business talking with you like this. I should know better. Now can you take my riding habit to the laundry room and see if you can do anything with it, for I'm bound to need it again in a day or so."

Alone, Sarah put down the hairbrush she had been toying with and looked intently at the silverwork. What had really happened to Jack Holland's wife? Could it be as Betty said? She looked at her reflection in the mirror and saw the blatant desire not to believe the story.

Outside the hunt was returning and she forgot the mystery of the late Mrs. Holland as she listened to the chatter and noise of her father's guests. She stood up and went to the window, hearing Hermione's studied tinkle of laughter and Edward's loud guffaw. The hounds were whining and yelping, the horses stamping and snorting, and the thought entered her head that there was a distinct similarity between the voices of the people and the noises of the animals. From the balcony she looked down at the ridiculous figure of her future husband, the Hon. Edward Stratford.

For the moment he had forgotten about his forthcoming nuptials. His full pink-and-white face was glowing from the exertions of the hunt and his carefully arranged Apollo curls were for once ruffled. The spirited red chestnut he was riding shifted suddenly, kicking out with a sharp hoof. Edward's tall hat fell forward over his nose and he was forced to put up his hand quickly to prevent the hat from falling to the ground. As he pushed the hat back into place he further ruined the stiff precision of his Apollo curls. He glanced around anxiously to see if anyone had noticed his appearance, but everyone was still full of the hunt. He sighed visibly; one had to be so careful; not a thing must be out of place, not a crease or ripple where it should not be. He winced as his stays pinched his cruelly restricted waist. Why had it to be de rigueur to look like an hourglass? The chestnut stallion was of a mind to be mettlesome again and Edward was forced to forget his appearance and apply himself to the matter of controlling his mount. Poor Edward, thought Sarah dryly; to keep up with the fashion he strove in every way with his looks, but succeeded only in making himself a rather absurd fop.

She turned from the balcony, closing the window and staring across the gathering of horses and people toward the opposite tower where a pale little face was looking down from a high window. Liza did not stir from her rooms when Sir Peter had guests. The girl felt Sarah's eyes upon her and quickly stepped back from the window.

Sarah looked around her rooms, listening to the sounds of Rook House. What would happen to her now? Lady Hermione would not leave this day's work alone; she would see to it that something was said about Sarah's presence in the wood with Jack Holland. Well, at least she did not know about Ralph. Sarah crossed her fingers in a gesture every bit as superstitious as anything Betty had done. She must hope that Hermione would tread carefully because of Jack Holland's importance—that was all she could hope now.

Chapter Four

*T*he whole sorry story was common knowledge; at least that part of it which Hermione knew was. Sarah had endured an evening meal which seemed endless and during which she had seen her father gradually become aware of his daughter's escapades. His gooseberry eyes had hardened with each successive whisper he overheard, for no one bothered to restrain their delight in the scandal. Unfortunately Jack Holland was not there, having left earlier in the afternoon on some business or other, for only his presence would have restrained the clacking tongues.

Sarah had watched her father drink glass after glass of wine, and felt his anger reaching out silently toward her. So far he had said nothing to her for after the meal he had retired with the gentlemen, and the ladies sat together in the withdrawing room, but she knew that it was only a matter of time before he confronted her.

She sat obediently in the gold-and-white drawing room watching the ladies who sat around like a group of bright butterflies in their colorful gowns. No one spoke to her but everyone spoke *of* her. She began to doubt her father's sanity in wishing so desperately to be accepted by these worthless people. Outside the winter night closed in on the old house and the breeze of the morning had become a howling gale which bent the trees. The rooks huddled together for warmth and shelter, and Sarah almost wished herself up there with them.

But at least this evening she could have no doubt in her appearance. The pile of Grecian curls had been expertly restored by Betty and were sprinkled with tiny lemon velvet flowers. She felt good in her high-waisted gown of yellow sprigged muslin. Nervously her fingers played with a dainty oriental fan; would this evening never end? Her nose tickled and she opened her reticule quickly to take out her handkerchief.

Conversation paused expectantly as she sneezed, and then titters of laughter broke out as everyone thought of the drenching she had received that morning when out on her clandestine meeting with Jack Holland. Indeed, everyone had wondered at Holland's reasons for suddenly accepting an invitation to Rook House. Now they thought they knew those reasons. Hermione's little eyes glittered. Oh, she had done her subtle poisoning well.

The door opened and the gentlemen came in. Sarah noticed immediately that her father's steps were unsteady, and his face wore a thunderous expression. His new walking cane tapped angrily. All through the port and idle male chatter which was meant to relax, he had been assailed by Edward's moans and groans about Sarah. The amount Stratford had imbibed throughout the evening had rubbed away some of the thin veneer of respectability and politeness which he always endeavored to show to the world, and now his temper had been brought to such a pitch that he lacked any discretion. Ignoring the niceties of behavior and manners, he stopped before Sarah and the abuse poured out in a slurred torrent.

As she sat there she could only feel immense shame that this drunken boor was her father. On and on he went, while his shallow guests enjoyed every despicable moment of her humiliation. Hermione could not keep her face from beaming and Edward's delight was scarcely less obvious. Now perhaps his uncle would relent and put aside this upstart wench.

At last Stratford's rage was spent and he stood there breathing heavily, his pale green eyes bright. She had made a fool of him, she and Jack Holland between them. All the social prestige brought by Holland's presence at Rook House had surely been undone by this. Stratford wished to be eccentric, wished to have his name talked about, but not in this way! He glared at his daughter. He had rescued her from nothing, from nowhere, offered her wealth, position and security! And how did she repay him? The anger flared again and he struck her across the face.

Sarah's head snapped back and her cheek flamed scarlet where his blow had fallen. Even Stratford's guests were a little taken aback at this; the smiles faded and looks of discomfort replaced them. Several throats were cleared and Hermione glanced around, wondering if her fool of a brother-in-law had gone too far. Sympathy toward Sarah was the last thing Hermione and her son wanted.

"Have you nothing to say in your defense?" Stratford nervously loosened his cravat as he sensed the change of atmosphere in the room. The wine-laden haze was evaporating and he began to realize the enormity of what he had done.

Slowly she rose to her feet. "There seems little point when I'm obviously already judged and condemned, Father." She inclined her head briefly to him and walked from the room, her slippers pattering loudly in the silence.

Outside her pride deserted her and she gathered her skirts to run in an unbecoming manner up the wide, curving staircase flanked by its silent carved rooks and rows of paintings of thoroughbreds. In the sanctuary of her own room she flung herself on the bed and wept bitterly. Betty came in and saw her, but left her alone to weep away her unhappiness.

Sarah's sobs would not subside and eventually she cried herself to sleep, crumpling the muslin gown and ignoring the pins which pressed against her scalp. The little velvet flowers were crushed and spoiled forever.

*   *   *

"Madam. Miss Sarah." Betty was whispering urgently in her ear and shaking her shoulder.

Drowsily, Sarah raised her head, her red-rimmed eyes stinging with the salt of her tears. Her head ached and her mouth was dry. In the fireplace a fire still glowed and the room was otherwise in darkness but for the single candle which Betty held close.

"What is it?"

Betty looked worried, frightened almost. "You must get up, madam, for there's someone to see you."

"Who?" Sarah's voice sounded very loud in the silent house and Betty quickly put her finger to her lips and looked over her shoulder as if expecting Old Nick himself to be standing there.

"It's Mr. 'Olland, and 'e wishes to speak urgently and privately with you. I didn't know what to do, miss, 'cause it's not right for 'im to come in here, especially after—"

"Where is he?" Puzzled by all this secrecy, Sarah interrupted the maid. She sat up, rubbing her eyes and straightening her ruffled hair.

"I'm here." Jack's voice broke into the room and she could vaguely make him out in the shadows by the door.

She took the candle from the maid. "All right, Betty. Wait outside in the other room. It will be safe enough—don't worry so." She smiled, but Betty looked unhappy, for if this should be discovered after all the other trouble today . . .

"If you should want me, madam, just call me." She scuttled past Jack as if frightened of coming within his spell.

Sarah stood the candle upon a small table by the bed. "Whatever is wrong?" For the first time she saw the paleness of his face and the obvious marks of a struggle which sullied the usual perfection of his clothing and appearance.

He came nearer. "A great deal, I'm afraid, Sarah, and the consequences of it will fall upon you and there's nothing I can say or do this time to prevent it." His voice was tired as he came to sit beside her on the bed. The copper of his hair shone as if polished by the swaying light of the candle.

At last he looked at her, his face strained. "Ralph Jameson lies dead at my hand." The words fell like icicles into the quiet.

She stared at him disbelievingly. "You cannot mean it," she whispered.

"Sarah, I didn't come here to jest with you. This evening I decided to take my meal at the posting-house in the village, having little stomach for your father's guests. I was dining in a private room when I heard a group of gentlemen enter the adjoining room. It wasn't long before I recognized Jameson's voice—he spoke so loudly that I think the whole village must have heard his every word." Jack paused, reaching out suddenly to take her hand in his. "Sarah, he was telling them all about this morning's incident in the wood, but he distorted everything to cast the odium on you. There was no mention made of his low behavior, no mention of his cowardly retreat—nothing. Instead he credited you with conduct befitting a whore. My temper has never been renowned for its steadiness, and I burst into that room and lifted him from his chair like a rat, calling him liar, lout, and many another name which I won't repeat before you. In front of his friends I told the true story of how he'd forced his attentions on you, and also I described the miserable figure he'd cut in his hurried departure. I left him no choice, Sarah; he *had* to call me out." Holland's fingers were warm and firm around hers.

"And?" Her voice was so low that she could hardly be heard.

He shrugged, dismissing the details effortlessly. "My aim was the steadier," he said simply. "I killed him, and so great was my fury that I had every intention of so doing. Had I come upon him alone I think I'd have choked the last breath from his body with my bare hands."

She shuddered, for something in his voice told her that he would indeed have done just that. He frightened her a little for she sensed a strange mixture in him, as if one portion of his soul battled continuously with the other. She clasped his fingers tightly. "What will happen to you now?"

"I came here before the uproar begins because I wanted you to know why I did it. I'll manage to survive all this, but shall first take myself away and allow the dust to settle." He smiled. "I'm sorry only for what this will do to you. Whether my version of the incident is believed or Jameson's, one fact remains clear: you were alone in the woods with him, and had arranged it so, and because of that he's now dead. There'll be great pressure on your father from all sides to cast you out and send you back where you came from."

"There's already such a move afoot, since Lady Hermione has told everyone that she found me in the woods with *you,* so my reputation will be worth nothing soon. I'm resigned to the fact that my days here are numbered, and in truth I think perhaps it would be for the best, for I don't really fit in this life."

His thumb was moving gently against her palm. "Oh, but you do, Sarah, you do. . . ."

The door opened and Betty hurried in, the draft of her movement setting the candle flame dancing. "There's a dreadful fuss at the main door, miss. Someone's there demanding entry in the name of the law." Her voice was round with alarm.

Sarah's heart began to thunder. They had come after him already. "Have a care, Jack." She used his first name quite naturally and did not notice that she did so.

He pulled his hand away and went to the window. Her room opened on to a balcony and far below the moat glittered in the darkness. Low storm clouds scudded swiftly through the night like an endless stream of dull gray steeds, and the wind rustled the ivy leaves which twined so thickly over the balcony.

"I can escape this way." He turned to look back at her. She still sat on the bed in her crumpled gown, her lovely black hair tousled.

He stared at her. He hardly knew her and yet she wrought such powerful emotions in him that, incredibly, he had killed a man for her. Quickly he went back to her, gripping her wrists and making her look into his eyes. "Is there anyone else, Sarah?"

"I don't understand."

"Apart from Jameson, has there been anyone else in your heart?" His fingers were hurting.

She shook her head. "No, I have never loved anyone."

His breath escaped in a satisfied hiss. "You shall, my dearest Sarah, you shall." He kissed her, murmuring her name softly as he slipped his arms tightly around her.

"Oh, do 'urry, miss, they're opening the main door now!" Betty's whisper was frantic.

Sarah hardly knew that he had gone. She saw his silhouette on the balcony, and then . . . nothing. Her heart was still thundering, but with more than just fear for his safety now. Her lips tingled from that single kiss.

Chapter Five

Sir Peter wisely chose to make his next interview with his daughter a little more private. The news of Ralph Jameson's death during the night had fallen like a thunderbolt and Sir Peter's head was not at its clearest anyway after the previous evening. What on earth was going on? Who had his daughter been meeting in the woods? Jameson or Holland—or both? Resentfully he stared out of the window of his study, rubbing the knee which troubled him of late. All his planning and scheming had been undone, and it was not his fault. Now he was probably further away from his objective than he had been before Holland had deigned to visit. But how to make the best of it all, that was the question. How could he, Sir Peter Stratford, contrive to turn defeat into victory? He was aware that his gross conduct after dinner the evening before had lost him sympathy. He was aware, too, that Hermione's triumphant attitude grated on him. He had always despised his sister-in-law, and her present behavior did nothing to alleviate an already tense situation. She had sought every opportunity to engage one or other of his guests in long discussions about Sarah's dreadful faux pas. Edward was scarcely less embarrassing with his continuous loud comments about his cousin—often accompanied by coarse laughter. The guests felt increasingly uncomfortable, and Sarah's dignified manner began to win her some admiration. The gentlemen in particular were inclined to take her side; she may have been born on the wrong side of the proverbial blanket, and she may even be a bit of an adventuress, but she had style! All this Sir Peter was aware of. But how to use it to the best advantage, that was the question.

He moved behind his ornate carved desk, his stubby fingers tapping impatiently upon the green baize. Curse this pain in his knee—like a hot pin jabbing him! His temper bubbled a little and he banged his fists upon the table. "Where is that damned boy? Eh? He was told to be here immediately after breakfast!"

Hermione flushed, flicking her ivory fan backward and forward with alarming speed before her hot face. Come on, Edward, this was not the time to flaunt defiance before Stratford. Like her brother-in-law she was determined to use the happenings of the past day to her best advantage, and her son chose now to be late! Her tiny, bright eyes swiveled to look at Sarah, who sat on a chaise longue, her hands clasped meekly in her lap, her eyes downcast. Hermione noted with some envy the long, black lashes and the perfect white complexion. What right had such a low girl to look like that! Oh, how she loathed her, how she *loathed* her!

A protective shell seemed to cocoon Sarah. The death of Ralph Jameson had set the whole house humming, but to her it was all dull and distant. Inside her little shell she was private, alone and undisturbed. She fully expected to be sent away, and was reconciled to the fact—and nothing on God's earth would allow her to give Hermione the satisfaction of seeing her weep. And so she sat there, staring at her hands, looking so demure, so pretty, and so utterly unlike Hermione in every way that Sir Peter found himself glancing at her with pride. Begad, she would have been a credit to his name. If she could have been presented at Almack's she would have been made—*made!*

The door opened and in sauntered Edward. Hermione closed her eyes faintly, wondering if her son had any sense at all. He was clad in a riding jacket of quite exaggerated cut and made of surely the finest and brightest lilac velvet in the land. Reeking of perfume he glanced beamingly around the room, banging his shiny top hat against his thigh, and slowly sat down in a chair, arranging himself perfectly. Even Hermoine stared at his trousers, for they were of the latest style, called cossacks, and his were the fullest, baggiest cossacks she had ever seen, gathered in at his ankles by brilliant scarlet ribbons.

Edward's smile was superior. Here I am, he seemed to be saying; you are back to me, Uncle, and this time I shall do as I like, lead my own life, marry where I please! Sarah looked at him with amusement. Had he thumbed his nose at Sir Peter he could not have been more obvious.

Stratford's face was suffusing dramatically, and Hermione was alarmed. Oh, Edward, Edward, you foolish boy. The older man stepped from behind his desk, clasping and unclasping his shaking hands behind his back, and came to stand before his nephew. Edward had gone so far as to place his long legs upon his uncle's priceless desk and the heels of his shoes were marking the polished surface. Quite suddenly and without warning, Stratford threw his nephew's offending legs aside and Edward sat up with a jerk, his mouth open with surprise, his face slightly comical.

"I say, Uncle!"

"Behave yourself under my roof, you young pup! You may act as you please only when *you* are the master here!"

Hermione did not trust herself to speak. She knew that Stratford could not abide her, so tactfully decided to leave her floundering son to fend for himself.

With mouth wide open, Edward glanced at his mother for assistance, but she was obviously going to remain silent.

Stratford turned to Sarah suddenly. "Well, girl? What have you to say for yourself? You've made me

the laughingstock of the district and I don't like to
wear a fool's garb. Which gentlemen did you honor
with your company in the woods yesterday? Eh?''

There was relief on Edward's face as his uncle's
attention was directed elsewhere. He fiddled petu-
lantly with his top hat.

Sarah roused herself and looked up at her father.
"If you hope that I'll deny everything, then I'm afraid
that I'll disappoint you, Father. I *was* there, with Mr.
Jameson, and then later with Mr. Holland.'' There was
little point in her denying anything, for the truth
would out sooner or later.

Hermione swelled up visibly. There! She was condemned with her own words! A sleek smile spread
across Hermione's lips and her little eyes glittered
like diamonds.

Stratford sensed his sister-in-law's reaction and
swung around sharply. Her gloating ceased instantly
and her face became a blank. He turned back to his
daughter. "Why?"

"Does it matter? Surely the mere fact that I was
there is sufficient.''

"It matters, for I would know the complete truth.
Which one had you gone to meet?''

"Mr. Jameson.''

"Why?"

"Because I liked him. He was kind and friendly,
and was the only one I'd met since coming here who
spoke gently to me. He sent a note to me, asking me
to meet him, and after a lot of hesitation I decided to
go to him.'' She swallowed, feeling Hermione's delight
exuding in all directions. Sarah felt certain that she
was to be sent away in disgrace and so had nothing
to lose by telling the truth.

Sir Peter gazed steadily and thoughtfully at her.
"And will you nine months hence have a tangible
memory of the late Mr. Jameson? Will you be as your
mother was before you?''

Sarah's eyes flashed with anger. "My mother very

mistakenly fell in love with you, sir, and I thank God she died before she could see what you have become."

He seemed unperturbed by the venom in her voice. "You've not answered my question, madam."

"No, I'm still as chaste as the day I was born! Mr. Holland arrived in time to save me from Ralph's advances, which, I admit, I'd have been unable to curb without help."

"Hmmm." He stared at her, stroking his chin.

Hermione was alarmed. The old fool was not reacting in the way she wished. The ivory fan closed with a snap. "Who is to say she didn't show her gratitude to Holland then, eh?"

Sarah was irritated. "In a chilly wood in January, in soaking wet clothes and with you watching us?"

Hermione sniffed. "I don't know how long you were together before I came upon you, and as for the wet clothes, well there are some who—"

"Enough, Hermione!" Stratford rounded on her furiously. "Such despicable suggestions are little more than I've come to expect from you, but now you'd better end them. It was you who made certain I discovered about Sarah and Jack Holland, with your embroidering and insinuating. Like you he was my guest, only *he* was important to me. But that didn't matter to you; you couldn't see further than your interfering nose! Can you not see how much the family's fortunes can be advanced by gaining Holland's support? Are you so dense then? Instead you gleefully spread slanderous tittle-tattle around until everyone is crawling with embarrassment."

Hermione felt the strings of control slipping swiftly away. "Stratford, you're forgetting that because of your precious daughter's conduct a man lies dead."

"I'm forgetting nothing, Hermione, *nothing.*" He stared menacingly at his hated sister-in-law and then at his lout of a nephew.

"Oh, I say—!" Edward felt that he must make some protest.

"You say too much too often, Edward, and now I wish to see your dandified rear departing from this room with some briskness. You too, Hermione. Get out of my sight for I mislike your face; it plays havoc with my digestion."

Hermione stood, her whole body quivering with disbelief. How could all this be happening? How could it all be going against her when that odious girl was so guilty? "And where does this leave Edward? Is he still expected to marry that girl?" She pointed at Sarah with her fan.

"Edward will marry who I say, when I say . . . or go penniless."

Hermione's fan snapped again. "My son shouldn't be expected to marry a girl who has caused such scandal. It was bad enough before, for she's illegitimate and no fit person for him."

Stratford's fingers were drumming his desk. "Be careful, Hermione, or I'll tell a tale or two myself about Edward's parentage. It seems I recall a certain Irish gentleman. . . ."

Hermione's mouth closed almost as quickly as her fan, then opened again. "That was all a scurrilous lie. . . . Your brother believed me."

"My brother always was a fool!"

Hermione gave in. "Very well, Stratford, but think on this if you will. It's hardly fitting that Sarah should remain here under present circumstances. You have guests of some importance—the Duke of Annamore comes next week—and her continued presence will be an embarrassment all round. And with Jack Holland's disappearance—"

"I've thought of all that. You may rely on me, my dear Hermione, to make the correct decisions. I bid you good morning."

With Edward trailing after her she swept from the room in an angry swish of mauve silk. The door closed on Edward's voice. "I say, Mother, what's all this about an Irish gentleman?"

"Be quiet, Edward!" was the sharp reply.

Sarah looked at her father. "I'll not be able to marry him, Father. Please don't ask me to."

He sat down in his chair. "He's my only male relative and will carry on our family name, so it's Edward or penury—the choice is yours."

The truth stared unflinchingly at her. Could she go back to Longwicke? To Squire Eldon? To be his housekeeper as her mother had been? Housekeeper . . . and mistress. Could she? No. She was not brave enough. She would cling like a limpet to the chance of wealth and comfort. Her new life was not pleasant and probably never would be, but the compensations far outweighed the problems. She was a little ashamed of her feelings in this, but she was no saint. Once in her life already, when she had spurned the lecherous squire, she had gone hungry and had known the terrors of being alone and penniless. It was an experience she did not want to repeat.

"Very well, Father. I'll do as you wish."

He smiled and made no comment on her decision. "That's settled once and for all then. You'll have to go away for a while, of course, but where to send you is the problem." He looked out of the window, massaging his sore knee thoughtfully. Liza was walking along the path by the moat, a pair of small brown dogs running around her, yapping and wagging their tails. He watched her, and a slow, smooth smile touched his full lips. It was a devilish smile which Sarah hated to see. He glanced at his daughter. "I think that Mannerby provides a most excellent answer."

"Mannerby? Where is that?"

"Devon. Dartmoor to be precise, a village right on the edge of the moor itself. Have you not heard of the Mannerby stud? The finest horses in England. The property has but recently, er, come into my possession, having formerly belonged to the present tenant, Paul Ransome. He lives there with his sister who will be able to act as your chaperone during your stay. I'll send word straight away and you shall leave in a day or so. I think anyway that I was mistaken in trying to launch you so quickly. You're not ready yet. Your previous life prepared you in many ways, as your mother showed good sense in engaging a tutor for you, but you're still lacking in that certain polish which is necessary. I'll use your stay in Devon to find a governess, a tutor, call it what you will, someone to coach you, teach you and bring you to that excellence which I know you to be capable of. Everything will be sorted out in your absence and Jameson's death smoothed over to everyone's satisfaction. It's a dashed difficult business, but no doubt can be solved. As for Edward, well, that fool can look forward to a spell of service in the army. I fancy it will do him the world of good. God help the army! Perhaps I'm giving the French a boost. I don't know." He smiled thinly. "But now to more immediate things. When the midday meal is served you'll enter the dining room with me. My guests must be made aware that you're still my daughter and still in favor with me. By the time the Duke of Annamore gets here next week I want everything to be as ordinary and normal as possible. With luck you'll be gone before his arrival; that would be the best solution all round. I'll write to Ransome now. You may go."

She stood, curtsied quickly, and then left him. She went to her rooms, hardly able to believe that she was still to remain in her new life. Everything was the same—except for Mannerby, and Paul Ransome and his sister.

Chapter Six

"Ransome! As I live and breathe, this carries co-incidence a little far!" Sir Peter's voice was both surprised and pleased as the butler announced the visitor.

At the top of the staircase Sarah paused, her hand suspended over the large carved rook upon the balustrade. Ransome? Could this possibly be the same gentleman her father had spoken of yesterday? She took a deep breath, swallowing a little nervously. What would he be like? She smoothed the apricot skirts of her day dress and then began to descend the staircase, the murmur of voices becoming louder as she neared the withdrawing room.

"Ah, Sarah." Her father smiled warmly, holding out his hands to her in welcome and leading her into the room; since the day before he had been almost suffocatingly loving. To her relief she saw no sign of Edward and Hermione, who reacted to Stratford's recent outburst in a circumspect manner which Sarah found even more difficult to bear than their previous attitude. They had taken to glancing meaningfully around at others in the room, catching whatever eye they could and holding the person in a stare of injured pride. Sarah preferred even their open hostility to this, and was glad to see they were absent.

Her father led her to the center of the room and she found herself standing before a stranger, a tall man with sandy hair and thick side-whiskers. He was somewhere in his late twenties and she immediately liked his relaxed manner and soft brown eyes. He was dressed well, in a dark gray coat and breeches, but never could have been called fashionable. Tall black leather boots and a top hat completed his appearance as he bowed before her, taking her hand in his firm grip. "Miss Stratford."

"Sir?" She knew that he must be Paul Ransome, but she waited for her father to complete the introduction.

"Ah yes, Sarah, this is Paul Ransome of Mannerby. Ransome, my daughter Sarah Jane." The gong sounded and Stratford took Paul's arm. "We were about to eat. Shall you join us?"

The newcomer inclined his head, stepping aside as Sir Peter bent to take up a pearl-handled walkingcane which rested against a chair. "A cane, Sir Peter? I trust it's nothing serious."

"Damned leeches can't tell me anything. Nothing wrong, they swear. Nothing wrong! Prattling fools— let them suffer this cursed pain for a day and then swear there's nothing wrong!"

"Perhaps it's merely the winter rheums."

Sir Peter grunted disbelievingly, and everyone stood aside as he crossed the room toward the door, turning to beam at Sarah and hold his hand out in an unbearably paternal manner. Coloring slightly she went to him and the party adjourned to the dining room.

Throughout the many courses of the meal Sarah's thoughts were mixed. She was relieved to think that her future guardian seemed so pleasant, that he was young and not some ancient ogre whose company would be dreadful. She was glad too to be leaving Rook House for the time being. She could not help thinking of her foolishness in meeting Ralph Jameson, or her incredible misjudgment of his character and intentions. Other, more unsettling thoughts crept into her head, too, thoughts of Jack Holland which kept her awake at nights. Her appetite was poor and she picked at her meal, her heart plagued with different emotions, but most of all filled with a yearning for Jack. She could see his red-gold hair and his dark gray eyes, the twist of his lips when he smiled and feel the touch of those same lips as he kissed her. Her spoon hovered halfway between her plate and her mouth and she stared at the white tablecloth, lost in her thoughts.

"Sarah, are you feeling unwell? I'faith you've nibbled at your food like a lovesick rabbit!" Tinkles of polite laughter greeted her father's words and she glanced up, startled. Paul Ransome was looking closely at her, sipping his glass of wine, his good-natured face pensive.

A blush crept over her at having caused such amusement. "I've little appetite today, Father." She picked up the crystal glass by her plate and drank deeply, as she had seen the other ladies do. The dark red liquid was heady and she felt its progress to her stomach where it rested warmly.

Attention moved away from her and she lapsed into her private thoughts. Where was Jack? There had been no news, and the empty place which had been set for him seemed to shout his name out loud; but everyone very deliberately avoided all mention of him. It was as if he had never been there at all.

Afterwards the ladies departed for the withdrawing room and their usual catty chatter, which invariably involved the tearing apart of someone's character. Sarah paused outside, watching them settle down like vultures gathering around a corpse. Who would it be today, she wondered, and the question was answered almost immediately as she heard her name and Jack's upon the eager lips. She sighed and walked away; this was one conversation in which she would not participate.

The butler raised an eyebrow as he saw the graceful figure of the new lady of the house slipping out through the main door. He shook his head; the master should never have brought her here—*never!* He sniffed and closed the door behind her.

The sun was shining brightly outside and all traces of the storm had vanished. Her shoes crunched over the gravel as she hurried along, and then she proceeded across the grass lawns toward the formal gardens. Tall hedges soon shielded her from sight and she went more slowly, walking happily in the warmth of the sun and admiring the beautiful precision of the flower beds and fountains. The gardens were at rest at the moment, but soon they would be full of color and life, and she hoped that she would see them. This thought surprised her, but then she would one day be mistress of all this. This was a notion which had not struck her before, and pondering it she sat down on a garden seat surrounded on three sides by a yew hedge. Mistress of Rook House. She glanced down and saw snowdrops growing in the shelter of the hedge. Bending down, she touched the delicate white flowers. Before her sloped the parklands, an ornamental lake with its swans, a cricket pitch, a huge structure of glass in which grew tropical plants, and away beyond that the dark outline of the woods where she had arranged to meet Ralph. She looked away from the bare trees and concentrated on the gardens instead. It was a tranquil moment, a blessed relief from the backbiting, vicious company in the house.

She did not hear the sound of slow footsteps on the path, nor the murmur of male voices. It was the perfumed scent of pipe smoke which alerted her to the fact that she was no longer alone. She recognized her father's voice and soon realized that he was with Paul Ransome. Should she slip away? But she knew that she would be seen if she left her seat, and her father would be cross, for she should be in the withdrawing room with the other ladies. She decided to remain where she was and hope that they would not observe her.

"What happened to the two fine ash trees which used to be here, Sir Peter? I see only the stumps remain." The footsteps halted as Paul Ransome stopped close by, just out of sight from Sarah's niche.

Stratford's voice was disinterested. "Edward had them cut down."

"Why? I remember they were excellent trees."

Sir Peter put his foot on the stump and leaned forward. Sarah could see him vaguely through the yew. "Oh, some bee he's got in his bonnet about them; he says they spoiled the view or something. I've quarrels enough with him as it is without making more by telling him he had no right to touch the trees, and so I let the matter rest. Still, now I come to look at the result of his zeal I'm inclined to anger. Those trees *were* excellent, and far from ruining the view they formed an integral part of it. However, it's done now and cannot be undone."

There was a moment's silence and then Paul laughed slightly, a peculiar sound, half forced and half embarrassed. "Had this happened in my part of the country then I could have well understood, for some say ash trees are unlucky, especially if planted near the house."

"Superstitious rubbish!"

Paul cleared his throat. "You said earlier that seeing me was a coincidence. What did you mean?"

"I meant that only yesterday morning I dispatched a rider to Devon carrying a letter to you. I could have saved myself the trouble of putting pen to paper had I realized you were in these parts. Why are you here anyway?"

"Well . . ." Now Paul's voice was very definitely embarrassed. "I was on my way to visit Ralph Jameson. He was by way of being a distant cousin of mine."

Sarah's heart sank. *Oh no, please do not let that be so!*

"Ah." Stratford's sigh was long and drawn out, and in her mind's eye she could see the owllike expression of understanding on his face. "And what you heard on your arrival set you scurrying over here with all speed?"

"Something like that, yes."

Stratford re-lit his pipe. "I'd no idea you were connected with the Jamesons."

"Oh, it's a very distant connection, as I said. I

wasn't in the habit of calling frequently. I was interested in a thoroughbred stallion he owned and he wrote to me last week saying that he was open to offers. I couldn't afford to miss his moment of weakness and so I traveled up as soon as I could."

Sir Peter decided to go straight to the point. "Come, Paul, let's not beat about the bush. You know of my daughter's involvement in all this, don't you?"

"I've heard bits and pieces, mostly conflicting, I might add."

"That's bound to be, bound to be." Her father was shaking his head sagely, Sarah could tell by his voice. "My daughter is a girl of little experience, Paul, a newborn babe in this jaundiced world. Jameson was skilled; he knew what he was doing and set himself the task of winning her. She was foolish enough to arrange to meet him, not knowing what he had in mind. Luckily—or unluckily, depending on your point of view—Holland chanced to be in the vicinity and drove Jameson off. Later the two men met up again and Holland heard Jameson telling a completely scurrilous story of my daughter's conduct and character. The result was a duel, which Holland won."

"Miss Stratford was most unfortunate." Paul's voice was polite but noncommittal.

"I trust that is your view of the situation, Paul, for I've a favor to ask of you."

"A favor? I, who am already so much in your debt, can hardly refuse you a favor." There was a slight hint of irony in the low, soft voice, but Sir Peter did not seem to notice it.

"Yes, I wish, as would any fond father, to protect my daughter from all unpleasantness, and soon there is to be just such unpleasantness over Jameson's death. Sarah is innocent of all blame and so there's no need for her to be exposed to any further shame. I wish to send her away for a while and thought that perhaps Mannerby offered an excellent refuge. Would you consider my request, Paul? With your sister being there too, there would be no impropriety. . . ."

"There's nothing to consider. I'm willing to offer the hospitality of Mannerby to Miss Stratford. Melissa has been there since well before Christmas, as you know, and frets much for London life. She'll be pleased to have some feminine company, I'm sure. Is it just your daughter who'll be coming?"

"Also her maid."

"I'll send word ahead to Melissa to prepare rooms, air them and so on."

"Excellent, my boy, excellent! My daughter will be ready to leave whenever you wish."

"I return tomorrow, but can delay my departure if you wish."

"No, no. Sarah will be ready then. My thanks to you, Paul." Sir Peter almost gushed. "I was going to take a ride—if my knee permits me. Shall you join me?"

"I think not. I rode up from Devon and have had enough of the saddle for the time being."

"I see that you rode the Turk. You take chances with so valuable a beast." There was reproach in Stratford's voice, a rap over the knuckles almost.

"I ride him now as I always have done. He'll come to no harm and remains healthy enough to sire a thousand offspring."

"Hmm, well I suppose you know what you're doing, but I don't want anything to happen to that animal. By the way, if the war against Napoleon goes well, I'll get that French stud I told you of before. I have high hopes of bringing new blood to the Mannerby stud."

"As you say, I know what I'm doing, and as for the French horses, well I have little time for them. You'd be making a mistake, an expensive mistake." Paul spoke brusquely, which surprised Sarah.

"A gentleman pays little attention to whether matters are expensive or not. It is à la mode to do as one pleases, spend what one wishes, and to ignore the consequences if they're unsuitable. But then, as you insist upon working for your living, you no doubt have little time for such sentiments."

Paul remained silent.

Stratford's grin could be heard in his voice. "Then I take my leave of you. When shall you call for my daughter?"

"After breakfast in the morning. But I brought no carriage with me on this trip."

"I'll send her in one of mine. I bid you good day." Stratford's footsteps crunched unevenly away along the footpath until they vanished from hearing.

As silent as a mouse Sarah waited for Paul to leave, but he seemed content to remain where he was. At last his footsteps were heard—but they were approaching her hiding place! Her eyes widened in alarm, but he did not see her, for he stopped just before the hedge. He was so near that she could make out the gray of his coat through the thick yew and see the shiny black leather of his riding boots.

She heard the long exhalation of his breath and the savage whisper of anger. "Will you never allow me to forget how much I owe you, Stratford? You have Mannerby; that should suffice without foisting your slut of a daughter on me! Innocent as a newborn babe, is she? If that's the case then I'm a Chinaman!"

Then he was gone.

Sarah stood at last, her hands shaking. She was stunned at the distaste manifested in that whispering voice. She began to walk slowly back toward the house, aware of Paul Ransome heading toward the stable block far ahead of her. She must face facts. Tomorrow she should be going with him to Mannerby and so would have to put up with his dislike. What an uncomfortable prospect that had suddenly become.

Chapter Seven

*O*n the morning of her departure Sarah was dressed by Betty with special care. Finally the maid put down the comb and brush and looked at her mistress in the mirror.

"There, Miss Sarah, you look a treat, honest you do." Proudly she touched a curl here, patted a tiny plait there, and generally fussed over the black hair.

Sarah smiled. "Shall you like going away from here, Betty? It will be a great change for you."

"Well, I shall miss Liza, that I will—'cept for my mother, she's all I've got. But I want to be with you, for you're so sweet and gentle, and friendly."

Wryly, Sarah pulled a face. "I've been criticized for that. No lady should speak so freely with her maid. The stalwart souls at Almack's would surely swoon clear away at such familiarity."

"I can't see what's so marvelous about that place. It's *awful.* I 'ad to 'elp out there once; Lady 'Ermione sent me. They stood around in their fine clothes talking, then they danced a bit, then they talked some more, and everyone was watching everyone else like a load of 'awks. And the food! Well, my mother would 'ave been ashamed to put out food like that. The lemonade was a funny color, the tea was almost cold, the bread and butter was curled up at the edges and the cake was stale! *Stale!* Liza went there, too, to attend Mrs. 'Olland before she was ill. *She* said it was dull, too. I can't think why they all want to go. There's much more exciting places to go than Almack's." She shook her head at the antics of the gentry and then crossed the room to open the wardrobe. "All these will be packed away soon, miss, so which one would you like to wear for the journey?"

Sarah stared at the bewildering array of gowns which hung in profusion on countless hooks. The finest dressmakers in London had worked on the new Miss Stratford's gowns, and the result was the envy of many an aristocratic lady; but to Sarah they presented merely another problem. Which was suitable for what? Which color was definitely not allowed before midday? Which hairstyle not suited to a particular kind of gown? And when finally she had arrived at the correct gown, which accessories did she put with it? Every day the same vexing matters arose, and every day she had to rely on Betty's judgment.

"Oh, Betty, *you* tell me! I've no idea. I doubt if I ever shall. Just make certain that I wear my mother's brooch—the rest I'll leave to you!"

Betty took the amber pin from the dressing table and looked at it, frowning. "Sir Peter won't like you wearing it; he says it's not grand enough for his daughter."

"It embarrasses him because it was his only gift to my mother." Sarah took a perverse pleasure in wearing the brooch before her father.

Betty grinned and chose a dress, and soon Sarah was ready to go down the stairs for her final breakfast at Rook House. How she loathed these meals and having to sit with her father and his guests; at least during the hours between she could hide herself away. But soon it would be all over and she would be on her way to Mannerby. She sighed inwardly, remembering Paul Ransome's savage whispering the day before.

The chatter in the dining room died away as she entered. She moved to the long side table and took a plate from the warming tray, inspecting the vast selection of dishes which steamed invitingly. As she lifted a heavy silver lid, the strong aroma of kedgeree drifted upward. If there was one thing Sarah could not bear, it was the smell of fish first thing in the morning. With a clatter she dropped back the lid to seal in the smell, and the sound was like cannon fire in the polite room. She closed her eyes, cursing her gaucherie which made into a nightmare even a small task like choosing her breakfast.

Edward was naturally delighted at this further exhibition of his cousin's unease in her new surroundings, and he tried to catch his mother's eye. But Hermione was busy with a full plate and ignored her son for once. Shrugging, he applied himself to his own meal, glancing now and then at his reflection in a huge mirror on the wall. The way he patted his bright golden curls was so narcissistic that Sarah wondered if he could ever manage to fall in love with someone else.

She walked toward her seat, not bothering to look at anyone. She inclined her head coolly to the butler who hurried to pull out her chair for her.

The carriage which was to take her on her journey rumbled to the front of the house, stopping beside the moat, the horses stamping and snorting in the crisp winter sunshine. Sarah watched, noticing that storm clouds were once again looming on the horizon. Two horsemen rode slowly up toward the house and she soon recognized one as Paul Ransome.

It was not long before he was shown into the dining room, where he took a seat and poured himself some black coffee. Edward paused in the act of touching his curls again, his eyes widening as he saw Paul's reflection in the mirror. He turned swiftly. "Oh, I say, *Ransome!* What brings you here? Er . . . how's Melissa?"

Paul seemed surprised. "She's well enough, thank you."

Hermione glared ferociously at her son and he colored, continuing with his breakfast in silence. Sarah watched with interest. What had her cousin said that was so reprehensible? Hermione looked ready to strangle him.

Sir Peter breezed into the room complete with new ebony cane from Bond Street, smiling benignly at his assembled guests. He was in an excellent mood and inclined to be garrulous, and soon the room was noisy with small talk. Hermione seemed almost relieved at her brother-in-law's presence and Sarah noticed how quickly Edward finished and took his leave.

Conversation drifted on, but Sarah suddenly paid attention as she heard Paul speak to her father. "They've found Holland, by the way. Or perhaps I should say that he turned up. He walked into Boodles club as large as life—caught them all on the hop."

Stratford nodded, a knowing smile on his lips. "I dare say. Well, now we'll see how much influence he really has! I shall watch events with great interest."

Most of the guests murmured agreement, for everyone was curious to know exactly how far Jack could go. Sarah stoically continued with her breakfast, pretending to be unconcerned and unaware of the glances she once more attracted at the mention of Jack. The toast was suddenly like cardboard in her mouth, and the apricot preserve tasteless. *Oh, Jack, Jack* . . . She bowed her head to stare at a slice of toast. She must be honest with herself, she thought, for she was more than halfway to being in love with Jack Holland. And what a hopeless love it must be, for a man like that would never, never do anything but toy with her.

The breakfast table echoed with derogatory remarks about their recent companion. Not one spoke up in his defense, but she noticed the dry expression on Paul Ransome's face as he watched them. He said nothing at all, merely sat back to watch. It seemed to amuse him to be a spectator at this particular theater.

She put down her cup with a crack and all heads swung toward her. She wiped her mouth daintily with a clean napkin and then stood, the butler not reaching her chair in time to prevent her from dragging it backward loudly. She surveyed the sea of faces before her. "Mr. Holland is in trouble because he came to my defense, and it shames me to hear you all talking about him in this way."

"Sarah Jane!" Her father spoke sharply, his eyes warning her to be silent.

"No, Father, I'll say my piece. It's not right that—"

"*Sarah!* That's enough!" Sir Peter's dreadfully quiet voice silenced her abruptly.

Paul Ransome watched her, and as she walked from the room he was the only one to stand politely.

Within an hour she was watching the final trunk being strapped to the back of the large traveling coach. Paul was talking to her father, and his companion held the reins of the two horses.

Suddenly the straps holding the last trunk snapped and it fell to the ground with a crash, startling Paul's black stallion, which jerked nervously. The man who held it spoke soothingly, and Sarah realized quite suddenly that he was French. He was small and dark-skinned, with a mop of curly brown hair and eyes which were almost unnaturally bright. Golden earrings glinted as he dismounted to steady the worried animal.

Sarah did not look back at the house as the carriage swayed down the driveway. She snuggled down in the warm blankets which had been spread over her knees, and wriggled her toes against the earthenware bottle of scalding water which rested at her feet. Betty sat opposite, leaning forward sharply as she remembered something.

"Liza! I forgot to wave to Liza."

"Don't worry. She'll understand how excited you are."

Betty looked relieved. "Do you think so? That's all right then. I'd 'ate for 'er to be angry with me."

The coach swept out through the stone pillars flanking the end of the driveway. On the top of each rested a carved rook, wings outstretched, beak open. Sarah glanced up and on impulse put her tongue out at the uninterested, unconcerned birds.

"Miss Sarah!" Betty smothered a giggle.

Sarah smiled, but the smile faded as she caught the stare of Paul Ransome, who had witnessed the entire incident. She conquered the impulse to put out her tongue at him too—but it was with great effort, a very great effort!

Chapter Eight

*T*he storm Sarah had seen approaching was not long in breaking. Only a few hours after the coach had left Rook House the deluge began, and the journey to Dartmoor was accomplished through the worst of England's weather. The rain streamed down in torrents, pitting the already poor roads and turning some into rivers of mud. The carriage sank axle-deep sometimes, and Sarah and Betty had to stand out in the downpour while the men freed the wheel. Sarah's morale descended with the rain. Was this a portent of the coming weeks at Mannerby?

The horses hung their heads low as they plodded along the muddy tracks which were beginning to climb now toward the distant outline of Dartmoor's peaks and tors. Sir Peter's coachmen were cold and miserable as they sat in their exposed position, and the Frenchman did not look as if he was enjoying the journey, for he seemed nervous and taut. Only Paul seemed unconcerned by the inclement weather, for his face brightened with each step which took him closer to his home, his beloved village of Mannerby.

The wind whined through the bare branches of the silver birch trees which lined the roadside and a new coolness crept into the air from the high moorland ahead. Sarah rubbed the misty window of the coach and looked out, pressing her forehead against the cold glass. Rivulets of rain ran down past her staring eyes, distorting the countryside, bending and reshaping it until she turned her gaze away. What use was there in looking out? It was like looking upon some landscape from Hell—a Hell flooded instead of burning.

The coach lurched unexpectedly to a standstill and she gripped a strap quickly to prevent herself from falling from the hard seat. The coachmen's anxious voices could be heard, and the shadowy shape of Paul's black horse passed the blurred window.

"What's wrong?" he shouted, his horse slithering to a stop on the treacherous surface.

"It's that stream ahead, sir. 'Tis too deep. The coach will either flood or float away. Or turn turtle!" The coachman's tone was doom-laden.

"It's Hob's Brook. It rises high on the moor and always floods swiftly when there's rain. Unfortunately there's no other way to Mannerby. We shall have to cross here."

"But, sir, the coach cannot . . . and what about the ladies?"

"I'll consult them now. Armand, take the reins for a moment." He dismounted, handing the Turk's sticky reins to the Frenchman, who looked thoughtfully back at the rushing, angry waters of the normally peaceful brook.

The door of the coach opened and the rain blustered in. Betty pulled her blanket more tightly around her knees, her teeth chattering. Paul looked in, his top hat glistening and his sandy hair wet and clinging to his face.

"The stream ahead is in flood and the coach cannot pass. You must make up your minds whether you'll wait here in the coach until the flood abates or whether you'd prefer to be carried across on horseback. Mannerby is barely two miles over that hill beyond the stream." He pointed with his riding crop and his heavy cloak dripped over the interior of the coach. There was something in his voice which antagonized Sarah. He was so disinterested in which course they chose, she thought angrily. Pehaps he even hoped they *would* stay in the coach, for then he would be spared their company a little longer.

She glowered at him stonily. "If we remain here until the flood abates I'd imagine the daffodils will be in bloom before we reach our destination!"

His brown eyes flickered. "Then you had best prepare yourselves to be carried across on horseback."

"By you, Mr. Ransome?" Her voice was as chilly as the rain.

"Yes."

"But what of the coach horses? Can they not be unharnessed?"

"Hardly suitable steeds for ladies, Miss Stratford." He was faintly bored by her questions.

"Horses are horses, Mr. Ransome, and I consider myself quite capable of riding a coach horse!"

"The animals pulling this coach are not in the same category as docile gray mares, madam."

So he knew about that, did he? She felt the telltale blush begin to creep across her face. "Do not judge my riding capabilities by the tittle-tattle you've heard, Mr. Ransome. Tell the men to unharness two coach horses for us."

"But, Miss Sarah, I can't ride!" Betty's voice was horror-filled.

The Frenchman maneuvered the two thoroughbreds nearer. "The ladies can ride with us, Monsieur Ransome." He looked at Sarah.

Paul nodded. "Miss Stratford shall ride with me." He glanced with a sugary sweetness at Sarah's stormy face, thinking that he had put her well and truly in her place.

The man was insufferable! Sarah's stubborn heart refused to accept his overbearing attitude. "Mr. Ransome, my mind is made up. I shall cross by myself on one of the coach horses." Her words were evenly spaced and calm, but inwardly she was seething with anger.

He gave up and slammed the door.

"Hateful man," muttered Sarah, but she was pleased to have needled him sufficiently to make him slam the door in so ungentlemanly a way. Well, her powers of estimation were proving lamentable when it came to seeing who was friend and who was foe. First there had been her father, who was no more filled with paternal love than was a slug. Then she had made such a dismal mistake with Ralph Jameson, and finally there was Mr. Paul Ransome, who was not at all as friendly and open as his countenance had at first suggested. He disliked her father and yet showed a falsely amenable face to him; then he professed himself only too willing and pleased to give shelter to her when in fact he was outraged at the very request. "Oh, Betty, I begin to shudder at what Miss Melissa Ransome will be like," she sighed.

She opened the door and stepped out of the coach—straight into a puddle which lapped eagerly at her skirts and soaked into her crisp white undergarments. Her shoes sucked loudly as she struggled out of the puddle and on to firmer land. Paul's face bore no expression but she could sense that he thought it served her right for being so obstinate. A coach horse had been unharnessed and the two coachmen exchanged glances as she approached. They were curious to see what happened next.

The Frenchman leaned down from his mount to touch her arm. "Please, madame! Let me assist you across."

She looked up into his intense dark eyes, suddenly disliking him. "No, thank you. I'm well able to take care of myself." She moved away from him.

Paul stepped forward and pointed down the track to where the creaming, foaming waters of Hob's Brook rushed and gurgled across the road. "Are you confident enough for that, Miss Stratford? Set aside all else and speak honestly with me, for I wouldn't wish any harm to come to you."

There was no antagonism in his tone, no hint of mockery, and so she answered with equal civility. "I can manage well enough, Mr. Ransome, believe me. But if Armand would help poor Betty—"

He nodded at the Frenchman, and then walked with Sarah to the bay horse, trying once more. "I beg of you—"

"Please, Mr. Ransome! The thought of riding bareback holds no terror for me. Will you help me to mount, please?"

He lifted her on to the broad back of the horse, pretending not to notice the inelegant and unladylike display of ankles, legs and underskirts which were thus revealed. She settled herself as comfortably as possible, watching Armand reach down to pull Betty up behind him. The Frenchman's eyes swung to her again, strange in their peculiar brightness.

She kicked her heels firmly and the horse moved away from Paul, dragging the bridle out of his hands, and then she was riding down the sloping road to the stream. The rushing roar of the swollen waters grew louder as she approached, and she gripped her knees more tightly as the horse stepped reluctantly into the foaming torrent. The force of the water unnerved it and its hooves slithered wildly. She held on for all she was worth, her face buried in the flying mane and her skirts dragging as the icy stream tugged at them. Vaguely she heard Paul shouting her name, and then, more distantly, a frightened scream from Betty, but she could do or say nothing. The horse was almost across, its muscles rippling with the effort. And then it was out, galloping along the road beneath the overhanging branches of silver birch, its fear and panic carrying it toward some woods which spread across the road ahead.

The still of the woods seemed to calm the terrified creature and at last it stopped. The rain still fell heavily and the trees dripped. Sarah took a long, long breath of relief, secretly pleased that she had not disgraced herself in front of Paul Ransome. The tired horse had stopped by a holly tree which was aflame with berries and Sarah looked at the tree wistfully, memories of her childhood stirring. There had been a holly tree at Longwicke, a tree just like this one, the same height and shape. . . . She glanced back along the road wondering where the others were. The wind swept through the woods and the moisture from the trees fell loudly to the ground beneath.

At last she heard someone coming and saw Paul riding the Turk for all he was worth. He reined in, the Turk's black coat foaming and steaming, and she saw that he no longer wore his cloak. "Are you all right?" He was breathing heavily.

"Yes, thank you."

He lowered his gaze uneasily and something told her that all was far from well. "Miss Stratford, I'm afraid that there's been a dreadful accident."

"Accident?" Her hand crept to her throat and she stared at him. What had happened?

He leaned forward to put his hand over hers. "It's your maid. I'm afraid that the stream proved too much for Armand's horse. It lost its footing and he was too late to steady it. They were swept downstream. I followed as best I could, keeping as near as possible, but when I found her she was dead. Drowned. . . . I couldn't find any trace of Armand or the horse; they must have been swept a good way downstream." He looked at her anxiously.

A whimper escaped her. Betty? No, it could not be true. He was lying! Frantically she kicked the heaving sides of the tired coach horse, driving it back along the track through the downpour. She heard him calling her but she closed her ears to him. She must go to Betty.

Hob's Brook filled the air with its rushing and on the far bank stood the coach, a dismal sight in the murky light of the late afternoon. The lamps burned, two small flickering flames to brighten the gloom. The coachmen were sitting inside and hastened to get out when they heard the hoofbeats returning along the track. In despair Sarah stared downstream as the splashing brook forced its way through the bending reeds and fresh green mossy banks. She turned the horse's head along the near bank, tears running down her cheeks as her gaze searched the far bank. She did not see the Turk come up swiftly behind her, did not see Paul rein in and follow her slowly.

Then she saw the sad little shape on the moss, carefully placed beneath a gorse bush, covered with Paul's cloak. The coach horse stopped of its own accord, bending its head to snatch at the springy moorland grass with its yellow teeth. Sarah could only stare across the torrent at that bundle beneath the gorse bush. *Oh, Betty, Betty, I'm so sorry. Forgive me.* She closed her aching eyes. Her shoulders shook with cold and grief, and her teeth began to chatter.

Paul dismounted and lifted her from the coach horse. Her fingers dug into his sleeve. "It was all my fault, *my* fault. If I'd not insisted on crossing she would still be alive."

He turned her away from the stream so that he stood between her and the maid's body. "You mustn't blame yourself. It was an accident." He lifted her onto his horse and mounted behind her. The Turk moved lightly away and after a moment the coach horse followed.

Sarah leaned her head against his shoulder, her thoughts in disorder and her sense of guilt overwhelming. She tried to look back along the stream but Paul's arm restrained her. "Don't look. It will do you no good," he said. She obeyed him, hiding her face against the soaking wet wool of his coat.

They rode in silence. Vaguely she heard the change in sound as they left the moor and came back onto the track which led to Mannerby.

"We're almost there now." Paul's voice seemed to come from far away.

She opened her eyes to look as they rode up the long single street of Mannerby. The village sprawled up the hillside, culminating in the only two buildings of note: the church and the manor house. On the left was the dull gray stonework of the church with its squat tower and tiny churchyard filled with dark green yews which overshadowed the tombs nestling in the grass below.

Mannerby House stood opposite. It was some five hundred years old, a beautiful, half-timbered building with rambling roofs and redbrick chimneys which had been added in a later century. Behind she could see the large stable block which housed the famous Mannerby stud. A walled courtyard hid the front of the house, and the double ironwork gates were closed.

Beyond the village were the vast heights of Dartmoor. The land rose dramatically toward those distant tors and craggy peaks which were half hidden in a swirl of mist and cloud as the rain continued to fall. One rock-crowned tor stood out; it was taller and more regular in shape than its fellows, and Sarah found herself looking not at the village and manor house, but at this single melancholy hill.

The Turk moved up the village street, passing the little cottages which huddled together. Paul stopped by the gates of the house and Sarah looked through them, seeing the great age of the walls and the ivy which crept stealthily up them, forcing its roots into cracks. The cobbles of the courtyard glistened with rain, and there was no sign of life anywhere. The only sound was the rhythmic tamping of the rain, and the occasional sound of horses from the stables.

"Martin! The gates!" Paul shouted impatiently as he waited by the obstinately closed framework of wrought iron.

From a tiny gatehouse, which merged so well with the walls that she had not noticed it, came a man so large he was built like an ox. He had a mane of carrot-colored hair, and freckles peppered his good-natured face. His leather jerkin strained across his broad shoulders, and he held a sack over his head to fend off the rain. He pressed close to the gates and peered out.

"Who's there?"

"Martin, it's me, Paul Ransome, and I demand entry to my own house!" Paul's voice was decidedly tetchy.

He was wet, tired, cold, and more than a little shaken by Betty's death. He was now drawing on the last vestiges of his patience.

"Master Paul!" Martin was rattling the large bunch of keys at his waist and the old gates groaned as they swung open. They closed again behind the Turk and Sarah felt almost trapped as she looked around the courtyard. There was rainwater everywhere, dripping from gutters into butts, pattering into large puddles, and most of all falling wetly from the glossy leaves of the ivy. Two bare trees stood next to the house: one was a lilac, and the other a tall ash tree which stood higher than the rooftops.

So this was Mannerby.

Chapter Nine

$\mathcal{T}$he doors of the house were flung open and a girl ran out into the rain. She was incredibly lovely, with almost white hair and vivid green eyes. Her face was perfect, faultless, and the pale pink woolen gown she wore suited her fresh, dainty looks. Hardly giving Sarah a glance, she flung herself joyfully on her brother as he dismounted.

"At last! You're back! I've missed you dreadfully."

He laughed, hugging her. "Keep your distance, 'Lissa, for I'm both wet and muddy."

Melissa looked at Sarah and then quickly away. "Where's Armand?" she asked Paul, smiling a little. "Surely you haven't traveled all the way on the Turk?"

Sarah could not take her eyes from the girl. She was like an exquisite doll. Her hair was pinned slightly, falling naturally into the Grecian curls which Betty had worked so hard to create out of Sarah's black tresses. *Betty*. The thought of the poor little maid pricked saltily behind Sarah's lids and she blinked the tears away. Surely it had not really happened—

Melissa touched Paul's hand. "I asked you a question."

"There was an accident at Hob's Brook. Miss Stratford's maid was killed and the coach and baggage remain firmly the wrong side of the crossing. As to Armand—"

"Yes?" The dainty voice was slightly sharp as Melissa guessed there was more bad news to come.

He cupped her chin in his hand gently. "Armand may be dead, 'Lissa. He was your faithful servant and I know not how to break such tidings kindly. He was carrying the maid across on horseback but the current was too strong. I found the maid's body but there was no sign of Armand."

"Then he may not be dead?" Her eyes were large.

"It's possible—without tangible proof there's always hope." Paul spoke reluctantly, not wanting to raise her hopes.

Melissa's lovely green eyes swung to Sarah, but it was to her brother that she spoke. "Then he'll come back. I know that he will."

He said no more on the subject, turning to lift Sarah to the ground. " 'Lissa, please take Miss Stratford inside out of the rain." He gave the Turk's reins to Martin, who waited nearby.

Melissa held her hand out to Sarah and smiled, but the smile did not reach those spectacular green eyes. "Please come inside, Miss Stratford." She spoke politely enough but there was a barrier there, an almost tangible barrier.

The servants waited in the hall to greet their master. The butler, Marks, stepped forward, a genuine smile of pleasure on his old, wrinkled face. As Paul spoke to each one in turn, Sarah could see how well he was liked and respected by all, down to the meanest scullery maid and kitchen boy. Yes, and by the adoring glances of the maids, he was not only liked and respected! He stopped to converse with the butler, listening closely and then giving some orders. Marks nodded, calling two of the maids and sending them scurrying up the dark, narrow staircase to the first floor, calling instructions by the dozen as he went.

Sarah looked around the entrance hall. How different Mannerby House was from Rook House. Both were old, but Rook House had been gutted inside and rebuilt by the finest architects in a gracious gold and white style which was more fitting to a new house than one so old. Mannerby was as it always had been, bringing a breath of medieval times to Regency England. Dark wooden bannisters lined the staircase and oak beams ranged across the low ceilings. Red tiles covered the floors, tiles polished so much that you could see your face in their uneven surface. Small tapestries hung on the walls, just as if left there by the original owner of the house, and everywhere there was the subtle gleam of copper and brass. A tall old grandfather clock stood against a wall, ticking the minutes away steadily and slowly, its face having a rather surprised look as if permanently startled by life. Ancient portraits were hanging on every conceivable space, interspersed by brackets which held thick yellow candles.

Halfway up the stairs, on a small landing, was a narrow window at the side of which was a huge portrait of a woman in Elizabethan dress. A stiff ruff framed the thin, hawklike face and she stared down her beaky nose at the group in the entrance hall far below her. On a table beneath the portrait stood a large, fat, porcelain Buddha. The Buddha was green, gold, and white and had emerald eyes which glittered as his head moved. From where she stood Sarah could hear the tiny chink, chink of that uncanny wobbling head.

Paul returned to speak to his sister. " 'Lissa, Miss Stratford will be happier in your care than in mine, so please take her to Mother's rooms. Marks is having them prepared now. Oh, and see that she has some of your clothes, for hers are still the other side of Hob's Brook."

"But, Paul!" Melissa's voice was urgent, "There's no need for Marks to prepare Mother's rooms. I've already set aside accommodation for our guest—aired and waiting."

He was impatient to be away, his quicksilver mind turning over various other problems which had to be attended to. " 'Lissa, Miss Stratford is an honored guest and so Mother's rooms shall be hers."

Sarah felt awkward, and the very last thing she wanted now was for Melissa to be offended. After all, perhaps the girl did not want someone sleeping in her mother's rooms. "Mr. Ransome, I shall be well satisfied with the accommodation your sister has—"

"No. You will have Mother's rooms, and that's the end of it." With one hand unfastening his limp cravat he turned away, hurrying up the stairs two at a time and calling the butler. The servants melted away from the hall and Sarah was left alone with the strange Melissa.

The girl's warm smile was fading rapidly as her brother turned his back, and she bowed her head coldly to Sarah and, picking up her skirts, swept regally up the stairs.

Sarah followed, miserably conscious of the poor figure she cut as she walked behind the dazzling girl in pink. She was made even more miserable by Melissa's obvious dislike of her. But why should Melissa behave like that? She had never known Sarah and could surely have no just reason. The Buddha's head tinkled melodiously in the draft caused by her passing and Sarah shivered.

Her skirts clung horribly to her legs and her shoes squelched unpleasantly as she hurried along the dark, beamed passageway. The light figure ahead paused, and to Sarah's surprise she saw that Melissa was somehow hesitant of going into the room where the maids' voices could be heard. The girl took a deep breath and then walked in, vanishing momentarily from sight until Sarah too reached the doorway.

The dull winter afternoon gave the room a chill look, but already a maid was lighting a fire in the hearth and the leaping flames sent out a warm glow. The walls were covered with a silk wallpaper painted with magnificent birds and flowers of Chinese design, and the pageant of delicate colors seemed to move the firelight across their dull blue background. A four-poster bed stood against one wall, a golden bed hung with aquamarine curtains of velvet. Everywhere was the touch of Melissa's mother, now dead, but obviously when alive a woman of taste and a love of elegance.

Melissa stood by the bed, her whole bearing one of nervousness. Occasionally she licked her lower lip as if it was dry, and her green eyes glanced time and time again at the window. Outside the rain still fell, lashing against the pane. The naked ash tree in the courtyard bowed to and fro outside the window, its branches occasionally bending so near that they scratched at the glass.

"Draw the curtains, Janie," said Melissa sharply and the maid, who was folding back the sheets on the bed, hurried to the window. Just for a moment Sarah looked out of the window and saw the tor which had caught her attention before. The curtains shut out the wintry scene and the firelight came into its own. Sarah looked at Melissa again and saw the relief which swept over her as soon as the curtains were drawn.

Looking at the maid who was kneeling by the fire, Sarah was reminded of Betty. She tried to force away memories, but to no avail; they crowded into her mind, painful with their freshness. She held her breath, walking to the fire and holding out her hands to the warmth. The tears were determined, but she was equally determined. She did not wish to weep in front of strangers, and especially not in front of Melissa who was so distant toward her.

The silence in the room was oppressive; she must say something to break it. She turned to Melissa. "Miss Ransome, my gown is so wet, perhaps you could find one of yours for me to wear until my own clothing arrives." She smiled in as friendly a way as she could, but her efforts met with a blank, stony wall of coolness.

Without even a nod of her head Melissa left the room, her skirts hissing like so many snakes. Sarah sighed and turned back to the fire. The maids and the butler had gone and she was alone. She stared around her at the hangings and ornaments. It was a gentle room, the choice of a gentle woman, she decided, and thought for the first time how quickly she could become at ease in surroundings such as these. Everything about the room was in tune with Sarah's own taste and character. How strange, she thought suddenly, that she, a stranger, could be so at home, when the daughter of the woman whose room it had been was so obviously ill at ease.

Upon the mantelpiece a small clock ticked quietly in its glass case on which was painted an ornate and incredible dragon. The dragon crept round and round the base of the glass case until its open jaws threatened to devour its own tail. It was a fearsome beast and yet in this room, it was merely decorative. Another Buddha stood on the table by the bed—a small Buddha this time without the shining emerald eyes of the other one, but it too had a head which wobbled when Sarah reached out to touch it.

She jumped as there came a tap on the door and the maid called Janie returned. Janie was a buxom country girl with wide blue eyes and neatly plaited, straw-colored hair.

"Please, miss, I've been sent to tell you there's hot water for a bath if you want one."

"Oh, yes, please."

"Very well, miss. I'll tell the men to bring everything."

"Thank you, Janie."

The girl dimpled with pleasure that Sarah had remembered her name. "The master said that I was to attend you, miss, if that's all right. He said that your maid had . . . had—"

Sarah nodded quickly. "Yes, Janie, I'd very much like you to attend me. I'm sure we'll get on well together."

The door closed, but soon the men were carrying a hip-bath into the room and a chain of maids came and went with steaming kettles of hot water. Janie stood importantly supervizing it all and then shooed them out, closing the door. She dragged a lacquered blue screen around the bath and then helped Sarah to take off her cold, wet clothes.

"Oh, miss, what a mess you're in. I'm sorry your introduction to Mannerby has been so awful."

The maid carefully laid the spoiled clothes over the back of a chair, unpinning the little amber brooch on the shoulder of the woolen gown. "What a pretty thing, miss."

Sarah nodded, taking it from the maid. "It was my mother's. It's all I have to remember her by now."

'Shall I put it safe, miss?"

"Yes, please."

"Here, in this little porcelain dish. That's where old Mrs. Ransome liked to keep her most precious things."

"Thank you, Janie."

Sarah sank into the warm, steaming water, closing her eyes with pleasure. How good it felt. She took the soap and cloth which Janie held out to her and washed her arms and legs.

"Are you courting, Janie?" She tried hard to be friendly because she felt so lonely, and missed Betty's chatter so very much.

"Oh yes, miss. I'm Martin's girl."

"Martin? Oh yes, I recall. He's the one who lives in the gatehouse."

"Yes, and he looks after the courtyard and outside of the house, tends to the garden, prunes the trees, and so on." Janie was obviously very proud of her young man.

Sarah smiled. "I wish you happiness then, Janie."

The maid bobbed a curtsy and went, pulling the screen around again to keep out the drafts which seemed able to creep in anywhere at will.

Sarah set down the soap at last and lay back in the bath, soaking deliciously in the water. She heard Janie brushing the clean gown Melissa had at last sent in— and then suddenly the maid was looking round the screen again. "Is this yours, miss? I found it on the floor just by the door."

Sarah stared at a heavy signet ring which the maid held in her hand. She took it, turning it over so that it caught the light of the fire. There was something familiar about it. . . . Her brows drew together, puzzled. Of course! It was the design on the front: a rook with outstretched wings—such as was found all over her father's house. But what was a woman's ring with her father's crest on it doing here at Mannerby? She turned it again and saw that there was an inscription on the inside: *My love is as endless as this ring. Edward. 1814.*

Janie suddenly clapped her hands and laughed. "Of course, how silly of me. It's Miss Melissa's ring. She brought it back from London last autumn."

Sarah gave the ring to the maid. The ring was Melissa's? Edward had given a ring to Melissa Ransome? Everything began to fall neatly into place as Sarah watched the dancing flames in the fireplace. Melissa was the woman Edward loved, the woman he wished to marry and would have married had it not been for Sarah.

Her head ached with the effort of coping with this new development. So much had happened already today without still more. What a terrible quirk of fate that she should have been sent here of all places. Was that, then, why Paul Ransome was so cold and distant? No, on second thought, Sarah began to doubt that Paul could know of his sister's affair with Edward Stratford. For surely he would never have allowed Sarah to come to Mannerby if he had known.

She stood as Janie brought a warm towel for her. Oh dear, why had her father chosen this of all houses? Practically any other place in England would have been preferable to Mannerby House.

Chapter Ten

$\mathcal{M}$elissa's odd behavior toward Sarah continued. Not once was she openly hostile, choosing to be bright and charming when her brother was near, and then sinking into a sullen, unfriendly silence when he was not. Nothing Sarah said or did could break that silence, and after a week Sarah was feeling inclined not to bother with her. She could so easily have told the girl the truth that she did not want to marry Edward, that indeed she did not even like him, but Melissa's behavior made such a confidence impossible. Sarah was now convinced that Paul Ransome knew nothing of his sister's love for Edward, and she had no wish to precipitate any crisis by anything she said. Paul was as distant and cool as he had been from the outset, and nothing would have made Sarah go to him with her complaints. So Melissa was free to carry on with her subtle goading, safe in the knowledge that her victim's pride was a sure protection against Paul's being made aware of what was going on. Sarah was left only to marvel that an exquisite girl like Melissa Ransome could fall in love with a lout like Edward Stratford. Unkindly she decided that it could only be because of the fortune he might one day inherit.

No letter came from Rook House. And, more important to Sarah, she heard nothing from Jack Holland. Two days after her arrival she wrote a small, sad little note to Liza, telling her of Betty's death. The letter had been sent as it was, complete with the marks of Sarah's tears, for she could not think of Betty without weeping. But at least she no longer had to rely on Melissa for her clothes. The coach had at last arrived and she had her own wardrobe again. Janie had as little idea of fashion and etiquette as Sarah, and so from the first day Sarah's hair had merely been brushed loose and then tied back with a ribbon. Gone were the delicate Grecian tresses, which Melissa's maid managed so well and about which Janie had no idea. Melissa had been slyly delighted with her rival's appearance, for Sarah no longer looked the belle of Society.

It crossed Sarah's mind several times to write to her father, explaining the situation and asking him to take her back; but each time she decided against such a course. Why should she allow Melissa to win, for win she would if she succeeded in sending the enemy scuttling back whence she came.

Seven days after the accident, Betty was buried. It was a single funeral, for they still searched the length of Hob's Brook for Armand's body and for that of his horse. But there was no sign of either.

As the bell tolled sadly, Sarah sat before her mirror tying the black ribbons of her bonnet. She looked angrily at her reflection. Her wardrobe may have been expensive but it was incomplete, for there was no mourning gown. Many long moments of discussion with Janie had produced this odd combination of a dull donkey brown gown and a black straw bonnet. There were no black gloves, no black stockings, and no black mantle.

"My amber pin, Janie. I think I shall wear it."

"Oh yes, miss, it will look well with the brown gown." The maid took the lid from the porcelain dish, but the brooch was not there. "It's gone, miss. . . ."

Sarah took the dish and stared in dismay. "But where could it be? I've not worn it since the day I arrived!"

Janie's eyes were large. "Oh, miss, I swear I put it there!"

Sarah smiled gently. "I know you did, Janie. Please don't be upset about it." She glanced at the floor, half hoping to see it there, but the carpet had been freshly brushed that very morning.

"But, miss, someone must have taken it then."

The words fell awkwardly in the room. Uncomfortably Sarah stood. "No matter, the pin was of no great value." But she was more upset about the disappearance of the little brooch than she cared to reveal to the anxious maid.

Along the passageway, Melissa came out of her room on her way to the church. Janie had just opened the door for Sarah and they stared at the apparition of elegant mourning which rustled toward them. Melissa was clad from head to toe in black crepe and her face was hidden by a thick black veil. The scent of musk hung in the air as she passed without speaking.

Janie caught her mistress's eye sadly. Miss Sarah was the chief mourner. In fact, she was the only person to have even known Betty, and yet Miss Melissa was sweeping to the church as if attending a royal funeral. It was not right.

The bad weather had persisted all week, but now the rain had dwindled to a fine drizzle which was blown damply through the air by the wind. Sarah looked down from her window as Melissa emerged from the doorway of the house, carefully rearranging the black veil. The ash tree scratched at the window as if it had fingers, and Melissa heard it, glancing up quickly and seeing Sarah's face looking down. But Melissa did not seem to be looking at Sarah; she was looking at the branches of the ash tree. She hurried across the courtyard and across the street. Sarah watched her open the lych-gate and go up the pathway between the yew trees in the churchyard. Now she would go down herself.

Paul was waiting in the entrance hall. "Where's Melissa?"

"She has already gone to the church."

He did not look pleased, for it was more fitting that the entire party from the manor house should go to the church together. But Sarah did not care what he felt or how he thought, for her single week under his roof had only increased her dislike of him. He obviously still held her completely to blame for the scandal at Rook House; she was convinced too that when he looked at her he saw only Stratford's daughter. She felt that daily he became more averse to her, although in what way she could not really say; it just seemed that each day he found it more difficult to be even passingly polite. As she put her hand on his arm to walk to the church she wondered yet again if she should write to her father, for even the prospect of Rook House with all its unpleasantness was preferable to Mannerby. At least at Rook House the resentment and dislike were not so very personal and close as they were here.

Martin was waiting by the gates, cap in hand. He was going to the funeral and was waiting for Janie, who walked behind her mistress. His smile faded as he observed Sarah and he looked at her in a way which made her feel uncomfortable. Instantly she wondered about her clothing, horribly aware of the dreadful mixture of donkey brown and black. Was it so bad that even Martin noticed it?

The street was muddy and puddles rested in every crevice. Paul guided her carefully through the water and then they were at the lych-gate. The slow clip-clop of the hearse could be heard and Sarah stopped, turning to look down the street as the black carriage came slowly up the hill, drawn by two dark horses with plumes on their heads. The driver cracked his whip slightly as they struggled at their slow pace. The plain coffin was unexpectedly adorned by a huge wreath of white velvet lilies which bobbed heavily in the glass-sided hearse, protected from the drizzle. Sarah stared. Who had sent such an expensive wreath? As the hearse stopped by the lych-gate she saw her own little bouquet, a small bunch of snowdrops she had gathered that morning in the kitchen garden. Beside the monstrous wreath it looked pitifully inadequate. The hearse creaked as the pallbearers lifted the coffin.

Paul was looking at the wreath, his eyebrows raised. "Your tribute is very fine, Miss Stratford."

She flushed, looking away from the coffin and toward his face, feeling that he was being unnecessarily cruel to jibe at her small offering. "I did the best I could, Mr. Ransome."

"Well, the result is most awe-inspiring."

She saw then that he was looking not at the snowdrops but at the wreath. "*My* contribution is the paltry bunch of snowdrops, Mr. Ransome!" Her voice was as bleak as the weather and she walked quickly to catch up with the coffin. He followed her and had no chance to make good his error. He looked thoughtfully at the cloth lilies and lace on the coffin. . . . If Miss Stratford had not sent the wreath, who had?

Sarah could feel her face flaming with hurt and anger as she walked behind the coffin. How dared he speak to her like that! She took refuge in her anger to set aside her embarrassment at both her unsuitable clothing and the enormous wreath someone else had placed on Betty's coffin. As she stared at the creation of white velvet and lace, instinct told her who had sent it. She turned to look at Melissa but the heavy black veil hid the girl's face from view. Even so, Sarah knew that those malevolent green eyes were fixed upon her. But why do it? Why do such a heartless, pointless thing?

The slow hymn died away and the congregation sat. The church was packed, for everyone had heard of the little maid's sad death, and they had all come. The vicar's sonorous voice began and Sarah clasped her hands in her lap as she sat in the Ransome pew. She remembered how gay and full of life Betty had been, only to lie cold and lifeless in her coffin now. . . . She swallowed and closed her ears to the vicar, who seemed far off and unreal.

A strange sensation of being watched brought her abruptly back to the present. Each time she gazed around, no one was looking, but she knew that the moment she turned away, those eyes would be staring again. The expression in those prying eyes was one of curiosity, and . . . more than that, of wariness; just, she thought, as Martin had looked at her earlier on. Perhaps they were all blaming her for Betty's death; perhaps that was why they were so cold and unfriendly.

Slowly she began to feel that even the vicar was giving her more attention than was required. As she concentrated on him she saw that indeed he did look at her often. His little eyes were round and each time he looked at her his nostrils seemed to flare with suppressed outrage. She felt more and more confused and miserable. Why was she being subjected to such unfriendly scrutiny by just about everybody in the village? She had done them no harm. Only Paul Ransome seemed unaware of the strong undercurrents in the church as he idly flicked the pages of his prayerbook, staring at the words without reading them.

At last it was all over and Sarah was standing by the freshly dug grave in the churchyard. The coffin was lowered solemnly into the grave and the vicar murmured the words, tossing a handful of earth which pattered on the wooden lid. He glanced up at Sarah as if she was contemptible.

An insane urge to shout at him came over her and she dampened it swiftly, but inside her thoughts screamed at the gathering around Betty's resting place. *Don't you think I haven't blamed myself a thousand times? Don't you? Don't you? Don't you?* The jumbled thoughts rose unevenly in her and she turned away, running down the path between the damp, dripping yews, and through the puddles in the street toward the manor house.

Janie followed, calling her name anxiously, and the congregation at the graveside watched with interest.

In her gentle, pale blue room Sarah lay on the bed weeping; she wept for Betty, for herself . . . and for the breaking of her heart over Jack Holland.

Chapter Eleven

*T*he next day was wet and windy. The cold air rushed down over Mannerby from the high moor, and from her window Sarah looked toward the tor, half visible through the cloud which clung around it. It was mysterious, like something seen in a dream and almost forgotten at waking. The ash tree tapped the window and she shivered, moving away to the fireplace.

The flames licked gently around the logs and she held her hands out to the warmth. Janie sat on a stool carefully stitching a tear in one of her mistress's gowns.

Sarah sighed unhappily and the maid looked up. "Don't let it upset you so, miss. They're good folk really. Mannerby's a kind place."

"Kind! If this is Mannerby being kind, then I shudder to imagine it when the place takes an active dislike to one! I loathe it here already."

Janie swallowed and lowered her eyes again, the needle moving busily in and out of the fine cloth.

The ash touched the pane again and Sarah jumped. "Why, oh why, doesn't someone cut down that dreadful tree?"

"It was old Mrs. Ransome's favorite tree, miss. She planted it years ago, when she was first married to Mr. Paul's father."

"What was she like?"

"A proper lady, miss, sweet and gentle. A Mannerby she was, the last of the family. Mr. Paul wouldn't cut down her tree, not even when Miss Melissa begged him. But then that was all Mother Kendal's fault—" The maid broke off in midsentence, her face turning red at having spoken so freely.

"Who was Mother Kendal?"

"Miss Melissa's old nurse." Janie continued sewing, but Sarah could see that her hand was shaking.

"And what was the nurse's fault?"

"Oh, miss—! I shouldn't have gone talking like that. It's not my place."

"But what harm have you done? I know of none. Come now, bring some interest to this miserable January day and tell me about Mother Kendal."

"There's not much to tell really. She's dead now anyway." Janie glanced through the window at the misty tor.

"You still haven't told me what she did."

Janie put down the sewing. "I don't know much, miss, and that's the truth. Mother Kendal was a queer old body. We village children were all frightened of her. She had care of Miss Melissa from the time of her birth. A proper country woman, she was, plump and with pink cheeks and a happy smile, but—"

"But?"

"But we were all frightened of her. She had that many dreadful tales to tell, of witches and hobgoblins, and things that would come to take you in the night. Oh, the bad dreams I've had on account of her idle talk! Anyway, she frightened Miss Melissa with stories of strange things being seen around ash trees. There were other things too. The upshot was that old Mrs. Ransome found out when Melissa woke up crying one night when Mother Kendal was away. The old biddy came back to find herself without a position at the big house any more. Mrs. Ransome was proper put out, to think that the nurse had been so unfeeling. Mother Kendal was given a pension, for she'd been with the family for years and years, and a cottage over by

Bencombe—not far from the tor you see from the window. She died a year or so back."

"And Mrs. Ransome?"

Janie lowered her eyes. "She died not a month after Mother Kendal was sent away."

"But Miss Melissa is still afraid of ash trees?"

"Mortal afraid. Well, I was brought to play with her, we being the same age and all, and I know how fearful she was. At nights especially. That Mother Kendal was a wicked woman. Still, when she died, Miss Melissa gradually stopped having bad dreams and things. Well, it only comes now and then, and always with the ash tree. The master was worried about her though, and so he sent her up to London last year, to his aunt. Did her a lot of good, it did. She looked that bright and happy when she came back." The maid leaned forward conspiratorily. "To tell the truth, miss, I reckon that she fell in love with some gentleman up there. And to tell you more, I reckon his name is Edward. You saw the ring—"

"Yes, Janie, I saw the ring." Sarah suddenly didn't want to talk about Melissa Ransome any more. "I think I shall go for a little walk."

"In *this* weather, Miss Sarah? But you'll catch your death—"

"A good thick mantle and stout shoes and I'll come to no harm. I'm no shrinking, fainting, London belle. Anyway, a bit of fresh air will make me feel better. If I don't get out of this house sometimes I'll become convinced that I'm not a guest but a prisoner!"

"You won't go outside the grounds?" Janie looked uncomfortable, for she had been told that her mistress must not leave the house and grounds unless accompanied by Mr. Ransome.

"I'll behave myself, Janie. Oh, I'm sorry. I know you're only doing what you've been told to do. I merely wish to take a little walk. Through the stables perhaps to look over the moor from the back gates. I like it there."

"I'll get your mantle, miss. Shall I walk with you, for company?"

"No, Janie, thank you. I'll be my own company this time."

A short while later, well wrapped in a voluminous mantle and heavy overshoes, Sarah slipped past Marks and out of the house. In the stableyard some of the horses had just arrived back from a canter over the moor. They stood together, steam rising from their flanks, and Sarah could smell that warm horse smell she loved so much. Her glance fell on the Turk, tethered to a rail. Paul Ransome was talking to the head groom, his back turned to the cloaked figure by the gate.

A wicked thought came into her mind, that, had she so desired, she could have taken any one of the horses and ridden out of the gate and across the moor. And a merry dance she could lead Mr. High-and-Mighty Ransome before he caught her! That would certainly be one way of livening up her miserable existence, and of removing the smug, overbearing expression from her host's face. She smiled to herself at the thought, but then the wind swept its chill breath over the yard and she shivered. Perhaps it was a little cold for such antics.

The church bell struck the hour and she turned to look at the gray stone tower, remembering the funeral of the day before. Had Liza received her letter yet? Sarah imagined her father's little mistress, reading that her cousin was so tragically dead. Poor Liza, all alone while Sir Peter Stratford entertained his fancy guests in the great rooms below.

She went closer to the gate, unnoticed by the men with the horses. Paul untethered the Turk and a groom led the stallion into his stall to be groomed. The hooves clattered on the cobbles and as Sarah climbed on to the gate to sit for a while the yard gradually emptied as each horse was led out of the cold. A solitary cat slunk across the open space, belly close to the ground, dashing into the nearest stable just as a groom was closing the door.

Alone, Sarah turned a little to look across the moor. The wiry grass rippled as the gathering wind sucked over the sloping land. Far away the tor was hidden in the mist and cloud now, but Sarah could feel its presence, looming high over the rest of the moor. She drew her mantle more tightly around her shoulders, thinking that her desire for fresh air was fast dwindling with each increasingly chilly moment. Seagulls swooped over the moor and she watched them. The sea was far away from Mannerby, and it must be stormy indeed to drive the gulls so far inland.

One gull winged low over her head, gliding on the wind toward some silver birch trees. Sarah's eyes followed its graceful flight, but then she forgot the gull. A movement of emerald green down by the trees caught her eye. It was Melissa Ransome. Sarah gripped the gate in surprise, for the girl was not alone. She was on her favorite mount, and she was with a man.

Sarah strained to see who it was. She thought for a moment that it was Armand. Whoever it was he was small and dark and rode as if part of his horse. He was riding away from Melissa now, back up over the moor in the vague direction of the unseen tor.

Melissa was returning to the house, so Sarah slipped down from the gate, having no wish to come face-to-face with Paul Ransome's unpleasant sister.

By the time Melissa's mount reached the gate, Sarah was already back in the house. Halfway up the stairs, she paused to look out of the window at Melissa dismounting in the stable-yard. Sarah's eyes wandered back to the empty moor. Had that been Armand? If so, why had the groom not come back to Mannerby?

Chapter Twelve

Throughout January and well into February, Sarah's predominant impression of Dartmoor was one of endless rain. Each time it stopped it seemed only to be gathering its forces anew. From her window she could sometimes see the tor with its crown of rocks, but at other times it was so covered in a shroud of mist that it was hidden from view altogether. She spent a great deal of time in her room looking out of the window, listening to the annoying scratching of the ash tree with each gust of wind, and at last she made up her mind that she would ask Paul if the tree could be cut back a little.

The rain gradually flattened the freshly dug earth over Betty's grave until after a month it was scarcely taller than the grassy land around it. The clean white headstone was washed daily by the downpour and so remained looking as new as the day it came from the stonemason. Sarah's feeling of guilt became stronger each time she looked at that sorry grave, for it seemed to be accusing her, like a painful wound.

The villagers were no friendlier than before, and of the staff at Mannerby House only Janie was warm and open. Sarah spent more time in her room, for there she was safe from everyone, and more especially safe from Melissa. She felt stifled: stifled by the weather, by Melissa, by the people of Mannerby, and by Paul Ransome, who would not let her leave the house unless he accompanied her. He was free so infrequently that she could count on the fingers of one hand the number of times she had gone riding since leaving Rook House.

Late one night she lay sleepless in her bed, thinking about what her life had become. She was more unhappy now than ever she had been since her mother's death. Everything had gone wrong, and she had not heard anything from her father, who seemed to have conveniently forgotten all about her. Not even a scribbled line about his search for a governess had arrived to soothe away her fears that he was going to leave her indefinitely in the hands of the Ransomes.

Miserably, she pondered on the invisible armor which seemed to enclose Melissa. The girl had so much she wished to hide and yet there was nothing Sarah could do to pierce that armor. Melissa knew she was safe still from Sarah's tongue wagging about Edward, and used that knowledge to her own ends.

Sarah turned in the bed, pushing the pillows and tugging the bedclothes closer as the wind wafted its cool breath through the house. The lacy shadows of the ash tree moved over the blue curtains around the bed and she heard the tiny tinkle of the Buddha's head. On the mantelpiece the glass-covered clock ticked quietly. The ash tree scratched at the window and Sarah's eyes opened. *That* was the only chink in Melissa's armor—the ash tree! Why, at dinner that very evening something had happened which made it clear that the formidable Melissa was indeed vulnerable after all.

Sarah had endeavoured to make conversation, deliberately choosing a time when Paul was present so that Melissa would speak to her.

"I'm so pleased with the beautiful room I occupy," she had said. "And I cannot imagine why you don't seize it for yourself, Melissa."

Not glancing at his silent sister, Paul had grunted, "She will not, because of some childhood notion about the tree."

Melissa had flushed then. "It is an ash tree, Paul."

His face was cold. "I'd thought you were over all that superstitious nonsense. You went to London on the strict understanding—"

She had smiled sweetly at him then, leaning across the table to rest her dainty hand over his. "I gave my word, Paul, and I promise you that it's all finished with. But I still don't like ash trees, and that's something I cannot help."

He returned the smile then, squeezing her hand. "My poor 'Lissa. And poor Mother too. She died cursing the day she ever brought that old hag Mother Kendal to be your nurse, filling your head with all that nonsense."

"It wasn't nonsense!" replied Melissa sharply, snatching her hand away.

"'Lissa, I'm ashamed that a sister of mine can so believe in country tales of magic and witchcraft. I'm having Martin cut back the branches for Miss Stratford. Just as I've often said I would do for you, but you would have none of it. No, you needs must have the whole tree cut down! Well, that tree was planted by Mother and it remains where it is!"

Melissa had then glared venomously at Sarah, who had brought up this whole subject in the first place. "And *I* remain where I am, and Miss Stratford is welcome to Mother's room—*and* the ash tree!" So saying, she had got to her feet and left the table, turning in the doorway to tell her brother that she would be going for a ride and would not be back until after supper.

Now, as she lay in her bed, Sarah suddenly realized that Melissa had not yet come back from that ride. The ash tree scraped at the window as if trying to attract her attention. She shivered. In the middle of the dark winter night it was almost possible to believe in its evil, as Melissa so obviously did. She sat up, knowing that sleep would not come for a long while yet. She pulled back the curtains and looked at the tree, remembering the trees at Rook House which Edward had had chopped down; that was all because of

Melissa, she realized now. Everything came back to Melissa, everything nasty and hurtful which had happened to Sarah boiled down to Melissa's presence . . . from the reason for Sir Peter's search for his daughter, to the wreath at Betty's funeral. Perhaps even the theft of the amber pin; nothing was beyond Melissa Ransome. Oh, how dearly Sarah would have loved to strike back at the beautiful poisonous girl.

The ash tree tapped and Sarah's hazel eyes flickered with a gleam of revenge. She slipped from the bed and opened the window. Down from the moor came Melissa on her brown mare, she would be back in her rooms shortly. Sarah reached out and broke off a twig of the ash tree, closing the window quietly and pulling the curtains across. As she did so she wondered why Paul Ransome allowed his sister such unusual freedom—and whatever did Melissa do until all hours, anyway?

Sarah's feet pattered across the room and very, very quietly she opened the door, holding her breath as it sqeaked a little, but in her adjoining room Janie slept on undisturbed. Sarah flew along the passage to Melissa's room, knowing that her maid was asleep too, for she heard the girl snoring as she passed her door.

Sarah laid the twig of ash upon Melissa's pillow and smiled to herself. Well, Miss Melissa Ransome, let's see how *you* like it! The main door was opening, and Sarah fled back to her own room, scrambling into her bed and pulling the bedclothes up to her chin.

Melissa's footsteps passed the door and went on to her own room. Sarah held her breath, and her excitement was rewarded by the sound of Melissa's scream. There was quite an uproar then, and Sarah lay like a mouse listening to the sounds as Paul Ransome ran to see what his sister was screaming about. His obvious annoyance and irritation was ample reward to the black-haired girl in the bed with its blue hangings. Let *that* be a lesson to you, Melissa! Tit for tat. Spite for spite.

It was not long before Sarah fell asleep, and she

slept well, pleased to have at last struck back, even in
so small a way. Outside the ash tree murmured in
the wind.

After her small victory, life settled back into its former leisurely, tedious rut. Sarah was forced to admit
that her triumph had been isolated, for she could not
continue night after night to lay ash twigs in Melissa's
room; and so Melissa was soon supreme once more.
She rode for many carefree hours on the moor, night
and day, even in the pouring rain, coming back with
rosy cheeks and shining eyes. Sarah felt more and
more that Mannerby House was a prison—and Paul
Ransome the jailer.

Towards the end of February, some six weeks or so
after Sarah had come to Dartmoor, she noticed that
there was a subtle change in Melissa. The girl's rides
had become more frequent and her manner decidedly
secretive. She smiled to herself like a cat with a mouse
to toy with, and occasionally Sarah felt that the smile
was directed toward her, that *she* was the mouse.

At supper one wet evening Paul had striven for
once to be attentive to his companions, and Sarah had
been pleasantly surprised at his warmth and humor.
He could, she thought, be quite charming if he tried.

Melissa sipped her wine and ate daintily, listening
as her brother talked of London and of the Duke of
Wellington's campaign against Napoleon. She evinced
great interest when he spoke of Prinny, or of the *beau
monde,* of Hyde Park, of Brighton and the new pavil-
ion the Regent was building there. But apart from
topics like these, she paid scant attention to his voice,
glancing instead at Sarah, who was listening to him
closely. After all, Sarah thought, I am going to be part
of this world he is describing and anything I can learn
will help me. Melissa was looking again and Sarah
became conscious of those green eyes. She is, she
thought bleakly, enjoying life at my expense. I don't
know how, but she is. . . .

Paul nodded at Marks, who spooned some trifle into

a silver dish before him. "Melissa, have you given thought to a new groom?"

She shook her head. "He may come back yet. Armand, I mean."

Sarah saw a sweet chance to make Melissa feel uncomfortable for a change. "Oh, is he not back, then?"

Paul raised his eyebrows. "You know that he isn't, Miss Stratford."

"I thought I saw him. The day after the funeral I saw Melissa with a man on the moor and I was sure the man was Armand. But then perhaps I was mistaken. Who were you with, Melissa?" Innocently, Sarah smiled at the angry girl.

Paul looked sharply at his sister. "You were alone on the moor with a man, 'Lissa?"

The green eyes rested malevolently on Sarah for a moment and then Melissa smiled at her brother. "Miss Stratford is of course mistaken."

"You were not with anyone?"

"Oh, as to that she is correct—in a manner of speaking. But it was most certainly not Armand. What reason could I have for meeting my own groom on the moor? And why, too, would he not return to Mannerby—if he was alive?"

Sarah smiled with equal honey sweetness. "Why indeed?" she murmured.

But Paul was not concerned with Armand now. He thought only that his sister might have behaved indiscreetly. "Who was he then?"

"Your friend James Trefarrin. I was riding back to Mannerby on the Bencombe road when I happened to encounter him. I remember it well. It was, as Miss Stratford said, the day after the funeral."

Paul was smiling again and Sarah was amazed at his apparent willingness to believe without question everything Melissa said to him. Perhaps it had been this James Trefarrin, but he and Melissa had certainly not been on the road; they had been among the silver birches, hidden and secret. Sarah poked at her trifle

thoughtfully, ignoring the drift of conversation as Paul
left the topic of his sister and the man on the moor.
The jelly wobbled and a whirl of cream slid down it
slowly. Sarah glanced at Melissa from beneath lowered
lashes. She felt almost convinced that it *had been*
Armand—simply because Melissa said it was not.

"Yes, how Holland extricated himself from that particular situation I'll never know." Paul's voice intruded
sharply and Sarah forgot Melissa immediately.

"Holland?"

His brown eyes were patient. "Yes, haven't you
been listening? I was saying that he was released some
time ago. I heard only this morning. All charges were
dropped and he is a free man, riding high in the Prince
Regent's favor again."

Sarah's spoon dropped and confusion took her. Jack
free? Melissa's little pink tongue licked the jelly from
her spoon neatly and her eyes were wide and so innocent, as if she had never heard of Jack Holland or of
his connection with Sarah.

Paul leaned back in his chair. "With it all blowing
over so excellently I have no doubt your father will
want you home again, Miss Stratford." He spoke indif-
ferently but Sarah could still feel that he held her
responsible for everything that had happened at
Rook House.

"I *was* innocent, you know!" she said suddenly,
hardly realizing that the angry words were coming.

He blinked with surprise. "I—"

"You have said nothing, Mr. Ransome, but still I
realize full well where you place the blame for Ralph
Jameson's death."

"Miss Stratford!" He glanced at Melissa. " 'Lissa,
will you leave us please?"

Without a word Melissa stood and left the room,
closing the door behind her. They could hear her humming as she walked toward the stairs. Paul looked at
Sarah's fiery face. "Miss Stratford, my opinion could
hardly matter less. I said only that I presumed your
father would send for you now."

"Yes, that's all you *said,* Mr. Ransome, but I'm no fool. You knew Ralph and you naturally feel yourself in a position of loyalty to him. I wish only to tell you that your loyalty is misplaced."

He pursed his lips and looked at her steadily. "Very well, Miss Stratford, you leave me no choice. I *do* blame you, fairly and squarely, for what happened to Ralph. Your little act has not fooled me for one moment. Ralph sent a letter here telling of the grand progress he was making with Stratford's daughter, and of the forward manner in which you behaved with him. What you told Jack Holland I don't know, but I do know that Ralph's story of what happened in the woods was the true one and that he died unjustly! Now will you put an end to this air of injured innocence, for I swear it makes me wish to puke!"

Sarah could only stare openmouthed at him, but at last she managed to find her voice. "He was lying in that letter. I don't know why, but he was. I did nothing, I tell you, nothing!"

He flung down his napkin and stood. "Madam, that's all I'd expect you to say!"

Her anger flared to match his. "And how can you behave so righteously, Mr. Ransome? If you believe all this of me, what on earth possessed you to agree to my coming here? You're a man of as little honor as you credit to me!"

The door slammed behind him.

Sarah's whole body was shaking and she took a deep breath to try to calm herself. She must write to her father—she *must.* She could not bear this any longer. The door opened stealthily and Melissa came in. Sarah glanced up quickly as she saw the splash of emerald green of the girl's riding habit. Melissa looked very lovely, and very menacing, as she stood there, her green eyes gloating malignantly.

The two women eyed each other in silence, and after a moment Melissa turned to go, her scarf billowing behind her. She had said nothing, given no reason for coming back to the dining room, but Sarah knew it had been only to look at her vanquished foe. There came the sound of hooves as Melissa rode out of the courtyard and through the gates.

Sarah slowly left the dining room and climbed the dark stairs. On the landing the Elizabethan lady looked down her nose at the sad little figure. The Buddha shook his head sorrowfully as the wind drew its breath. Outside it had begun to rain again and Sarah stood by the window and gazed out. The glass misted as the rain dashed against it.

Hoofbeats sounded again and she looked out. Was Melissa coming back already? She strained her eyes against the semi-darkness and the weather.

A solitary horseman was riding past the house on his way to the moor. A shaft of light from Martin's gatehouse momentarily rested on the bright chestnut flank of his horse. The man was hunched against the weather, his top hat pulled down over his face. He was very fashionable, that much Sarah could see, with his high, high collar. His voluminous cravat billowed in the wind. She watched until he was out of sight and then walked on to her room.

She sat by her dressing table quietly while Janie untied her ribbon and began to brush her hair. She thought of Jack and forgot all about the letter she wished to write.

He was free. Would she ever see him again? Would he maybe come to see her? Would he even want to know her after all that had happened?

She closed her eyes as the brush worked gently and soothingly. His kiss seemed to burn on her lips even now. *Oh Jack, don't forget me, don't forget me. . . .*

Chapter Thirteen

*T*he following day dawned bright and clear. The moor was golden on this first day of March, and from Sarah's window everything looked warm and springlike. The ash tree spread its branches like bars across the window, but since Martin had trimmed it early that morning it could no longer touch the glass. The tor shimmered in the distance, swaying in the haze. As Sarah prepared to go down to breakfast she felt her imprisonment acutely and resentment waxed strongly in her heart.

"There, miss, you look very nice. Blue suits you so." Janie smiled at her in the mirror, putting the finishing touches to the bow which held Sarah's thick black hair back.

"And who is there to notice how I look, Janie? Mr. Ransome? I think not. He wouldn't notice if I sat down to breakfast in my undergown."

"Miss Sarah!" Janie was horrified that her mistress could even think such a dreadful thing.

Sarah's expression was wry. "Indeed, when I think of it, I imagine he would be completely unsurprised by my doing such a thing, for so low is his opinion of me that he doubtless thinks I make a habit of such behavior!"

She picked up her reticule and went to the door. As she opened it Paul and Melissa were walking along the passage, and they stopped. Melissa smiled sweetly. "Good morning, Sarah. I trust that the storm did not keep you awake last night." Even the sweetness in her voice sounded so utterly believable.

Sarah returned the smile woodenly. "I slept well, thank you."

Paul glanced at her. What ailed the woman? She looked peaky. Or was she still sulking because of what he had said the night before? "Are you all right, Miss Stratford?" he inquired.

"I'm well enough, Mr. Ransome,"

"You look pale . . . er, unwell."

Melissa's laugh tinkled out. "Oh, tush, Paul, did you not know that to look pale and unwell is *the* look this Season? Shame on you for being so ungallant." Her wide green eyes looked spitefully at Sarah's unfashionably tied hair and then she patted her own cascade of white Grecian curls.

Paul grunted. " 'Lissa, I trust that this Season's languid look applies only to those of a healthy disposition. Miss Stratford looks unwell to me, and it's not ungallant to ask." He looked anew at Sarah. "I'd rather you gave me a truthful answer, Miss Stratford."

She looked rebellious. She *did* feel unwell—who would not, being cooped up in this odious house with only his odious self and his equally odious sister for companions! "I feel suffocated for lack of good fresh air, Mr. Ransome. I'd ask you to permit me a measure of freedom—such as you permit your sister."

"I cannot allow you to ride alone whenever and wherever you please, Miss Stratford. You must see that."

"I'm afraid that I do not, Mr. Ransome. If Melissa needs no supervision then I fail to see why I do." She was desperate to be free of Mannerby House, and free of Paul Ransome.

"Miss Stratford, my sister is here of her own volition. This is her home. You, on the other hand, have been sent here under circumstances which give me cause to severely curtail your freedom while under my protection."

Flame red scorched across her pale face at these words. What a toad the man was! "Mr. Ransome, for once I find myself in agreement with your sister. You *are* ungallant!" Shaking with emotion, she shut the door in his face and turned to look at Janie who had overheard everything.

She went to the chair by the window, sitting down with so dark a face that Janie remained silent. Sarah opened the window. Outside, the village street rang with noise and bustle as the people went about their business. Wisps of smoke rose from the chimneys and there was a delicious smell of fresh baked bread. Sarah's stomach reminded her sharply that she had not eaten—nor would she now after her display of temper!

Down the slope of the hillside she looked at the dark strip of the woods through which she had ridden on her journey from Rook House. The trees were still bare, but now their grayness was mellowed by the sunshine, and she could imagine the softness of the moss beneath a horse's hooves. Oh, how she longed for a ride! A tiny speck of chestnut moved along the edge of the wood and she leaned forward. A horseman was there, his face turned toward the village. As she looked he melted into the woods. She was puzzled, for she recognized the bright chestnut horse as the one she had seen the previous evening.

Across the room she could see her reflection in the mirror. Her eyes were dark-rimmed, tired, and anxious. Her hair was dull and her skin was so pale as to be almost white, which, although it may have been the very height of fashion, did little for Sarah. She needed a touch of color, a sparkle in her eyes and a sheen in her hair. Paul Ransome was right after all; she did look unwell. She pulled a face at herself.

"Miss Stratford, may I come in?"

Startled she turned in her chair to see Paul standing in the doorway. She felt foolish, knowing that he had probably witnessed her face-pulling.

"Miss Stratford, I think your anger with my ill manners was justified and I've come to offer my apologies, and to make amends, if I may." His words were not stilted and he looked genuinely sorry.

"I accept your apology, Mr. Ransome." Try as she would, Sarah could not be gracious.

He sighed. "Then you would not relish the thought of a ride after all? And on such a magnificent day too—still . . ." He began to turn away but she almost ran across the room to him, putting her hand on his arm.

He glanced down at her hand and she removed it immediately. She bit her lip. "Mr. Ransome, I *would* relish a ride. Yes, indeed I would. Let us be honest with each other. You don't like me, and I do assure you that the feeling is mutual. I can only say again that I don't deserve your dislike. However, I'm under your roof and must remain here until my father sees fit to send for me. Until then I would wish to live as peacefully as possible. I'd love to go for a ride. Thank you so much for asking me." She finished this long speech with a rush and watched him anxiously.

He nodded. "Be ready to leave within the hour, Miss Stratford. Melissa will accompany us." He left the room, closing the door as quietly as he had opened it.

Janie cleared her throat. "Shall I put out your riding things, miss?"

"Yes, thank you, Janie. Oh, how good it will be to get out and away from this house with its awful atmosphere."

The maid looked a little agitated at her words. "I've been wanting to speak with you about that, miss, but didn't know quite what to say. I know that no one likes you or trusts you, and I don't know why. You're such a dear lady and have done nothing to deserve their spite. Even Martin acts as if you are bad and he doesn't like it one bit that I'm your maid, but he won't tell me why he dislikes you so much because he knows *I* like you."

Sarah smiled. "And I like you, Janie, and thank you for your concern and loyalty."

"It's not so simple, miss, because their feeling is so powerful. They think you've done something awful."

Sarah closed her eyes for a moment. Betty. It must be Betty's death. And perhaps Ralph's death too . . .

Janie took out the wine red velvet riding habit and laid it on the bed. "Just be careful, Miss Sarah, that's all, for I don't like it one little bit."

"Yes, Janie." Sarah turned for the maid to unhook her blue woolen gown. "Oh, Janie, I wish to write a letter when I return from this ride. Can you arrange to post it for me . . . without Mr. Ransome or his sister knowing? I'd rather they didn't find out that I'd written to my father."

"Yes, miss, just you leave it to me."

A short while later Sarah descended to the drawing room where Paul Ransome was already waiting. "You look most charming, Miss Stratford," he said politely.

"Thank you, Mr. Ransome," she replied in equally polite tone.

"Paul? Am I late?" Melissa came hurrying down the stairs in a flurry of emerald green. She glowed, and Sarah felt suddenly dull beside such sparkling vitality. It was with some satisfaction that she noticed a tear at the base of Melissa's riding skirt; well, at least there was something to mar that dreadfully complete perfection!

Paul put on his top hat. "I thought we would ride to Bencombe."

Melissa's face fell. "Oh no, Paul, let's go somewhere else."

He smiled. "I'm afraid that I've some business there, for I must see James Trefarrin."

"That man! I don't like him!" Melissa was obviously upset in some way, and Sarah looked at her in surprise.

Paul smiled affectionately at his sister. "I'm sure that James would be heartbroken to see you look like that at the prospect of meeting him, 'Lissa. Come on, now, for Bencombe is a far ride and perhaps we can eat at James's excellent hostelry."

Outside in the courtyard three horses waited. Sarah breathed deeply of the fresh moorland air and smiled at the groom who held her mount, but he would not meet her eyes.

A tiny black-and-white dog with a black patch over one eye hurtled unexpectedly across the courtyard toward Paul, yapping frantically and wagging its stumpy little tail. With a yelp of delight it flung itself upon him, licking his face and almost knocking his hat from his head. Paul was laughing as he held the little creature. "Kitty! You rascal!" He ruffled the floppy ears and rubbed the furry head which butted constantly against his hand.

Martin came hurrying up, panting and dismayed at his dog's behavior. "I'm sorry, sir. I tried to hold her back."

"That's all right, Martin. It's good to see her out and about again. How are her pups? Do they flourish?"

"Aye, that they do, sir. A fine handful they'll be soon."

Sarah was interested. "Has she some puppies then, Martin?"

He glanced at her quickly and then away. "Yes, miss, six of them."

"May I see them please?"

He was reluctant. "Well, miss . . ."

Paul put the excited dog on the cobbles. "Come now, Martin, it's a small request. Perhaps afterwards you could show Miss Stratford how well Kitty dances a jig."

"Yes, sir."

Sarah remembered what Janie had said such a short time before. Martin quite obviously did not like Mr. Ransome's guest.

They walked across the courtyard toward the gatehouse, and Kitty danced around them on dainty paws. The puppies were small and round, with their eyes

still closed, and each one was a black-and-white minia-
ture of its mother. Kitty sat down with them proudly
and Sarah laughed. "Look at her. She's as proud as
any fine lady showing off her firstborn." She stroked
the dog and Kitty licked her hand.

"You are fond of dogs?" Paul crouched down beside her, touching the tiny furry bundles in the straw.

"Oh yes, I had one of my own once." It was long
since she had thought of her childhood pet.

Paul looked at her profile and then up at Martin.
"Martin, when they're old enough perhaps you'll give
one to Miss Stratford. . . ."

"They're all spoken for, sir," the big man spoke
hurriedly.

Paul was surprised. "What, all of them? Who
around here wants them?"

"They're all spoken for," repeated Martin, staring
at the puppies firmly.

He just doesn't want me to have one, thought Sarah.
The puppies were not spoken for, she knew that, and
so did Paul, who merely shrugged.

"Well, at least Kitty's dancing time isn't spoken for.
Come on, Martin, get out your fiddle and let Kitty
entertain us."

Never before had Sarah seen a dog dance a jig, but
Kitty did. She tottered around on her hind legs as
Martin scraped out a tune on his ancient fiddle. Kitty
reveled in all the attention she was getting and danced
as finely as any actress on the stage in London. Sarah
was captivated as she watched, and her eyes shone.
Paul studied her; it was hard to believe that this girl
who took such a delight in Kitty's puppies and in the
little dog's dancing antics could have been capable of
such heartless behavior at Rook House. . . .

The foot-tapping music ended with a loud chord and
Kitty dropped to all fours, tail still wagging. Paul bent
to pat the dog's head before turning to the two
women. "Well, ladies, I think we must go now."

"Let's go somewhere other than Bencombe, Paul,"
pleaded Melissa for the last time.

"No, 'Lissa. Bencombe it is," he said firmly, crossing the courtyard to mount the Turk.

Melissa followed him, her expression apprehensive.

When they rode up from the village and on to the moor itself, Sarah found herself speechless at its magnificence. The rolling, wildly beautiful land stretched ahead for miles, covered with the brown bracken of last year and the new heather leaves of the present year. Silver birch trees dotted the green carpet in every direction, and rocks and boulders were scattered as if by some giant hand. Now and then the land rose steeply to a tor, but high above all others was Sarah's tor—Hob's Tor she now knew it to be named, where Hob's Brook rose. Everything basked in the sunshine. Dimples in the ground marked the passage of tiny streams, and from overhead came the lonely calls of the curlews. The blue skies were free of all clouds, and there was no wind to chill the air. A hawk hovered momentarily, before plummeting down to the heather to grasp some prey.

Sarah rode on through the morning splendor, oblivious to the awkward sidesaddle. She absorbed the magic of Dartmoor. Ponies grazed on the lower slopes of a hill—splashes of gray, chestnut, and bay against the moor. Further away a small flock of sheep moved slowly along a ridge, surefooted and unconcerned.

Paul looked at Sarah's rapt face. "You seem lost to the moor."

"I am. It's surely the most wonderful sight I've ever seen."

"Yes, and one which never palls."

"Were you born here, Mr. Ransome?"

"I was, and have always lived here. Mannerby House has been in my family since it was first built. My mother was a Mannerby; the family name died out with her." He looked away quickly and she remembered that he no longer owned Mannerby. She wondered, not for the first time, what had forced him to sell the place to her father, whom he clearly did not like.

The small market town of Bencombe nestled in a fold in the moor. In the square was the sign of the Blue Fox, a beautiful Tudor building with tall gables and chimneys, and a half-timbered frontage. It had ancient bow windows with thick, uneven glass panes which obscured the interior of the inn. Paul led the way into the galleried yard behind and the sound of their horses brought James Trefarrin hurrying out to greet them. One glance at the inkeeper told Sarah that he most certainly was not the small, dark man she had seen with Melissa.

"Mr. Ransome, Mr. Ransome, what an honor it is, an honor indeed." The man wiped his hands on his impeccable white apron, bowing as he spoke. He was Paul's age, stocky, with a prematurely balding head, a large paunch and freckles on his red nose.

"Well, James, I trust your hostelry has fare fit for us." Paul dismounted, giving the Turk's reins to a groom and holding out his hand to the innkeeper, who seized and shook it gladly.

"My inn can compete with any of your fancy London places—if that thieving vagabond by Hob's Tor leaves my supply of mutton alone."

"Vagabond? What's all this?"

"Oh, some fellow hiding up there. They reckon perhaps in the old cave where— Anyway, no one will go up and look, not to that old place. But if he doesn't stop soon we'll have to get together and flush him out somehow—though who would come with me to that cursed place I don't know. He's had at least four sheep from my enclosure and the new folk in Mother Kendal's old cottage have talked of losing eggs from the coops."

Paul's smile faded a little. "I'll warrant if the old witch herself was still alive no one would ever dare steal her eggs."

"Ah, well, Mother Kendal may be gone but her memory is fearsome enough. Her haunts are still avoided as surely as ever they were."

"James, she's dead, and so are most of her cronies,

and those that remain have set that aside once and for all. Hob's Tor holds no terror for me. I'll help you seek out your thieving vagabond."

James grinned broadly. "Reckon Old Nick himself would be sent running from you and me, Master Paul."

"Aye, pitchfork and all!"

Trefarrin looked past Paul to where some ostlers were trying to control a nervous horse which had no intention of standing between the shafts of a cart. "Have a care, you dolts. That's best Froggie cognac there." He grinned at Paul, rubbing his finger against the side of his nose, "The best the Revenue men have missed! And talking of Froggies, I reckon I saw that groom we all thought was drowned in Hob's Brook. Early one morning a day or so back. I was up because my rheumatism was playing me foolish again. If it wasn't him then it was someone just like him. Riding south he was, toward Mannerby."

Sarah glanced quickly at Melissa, but the girl did not move a muscle. Paul merely shrugged. "It seems everyone is seeing Armand at every corner. I fear the poor man is dead. Unless, of course, he's afraid to return to us in case he is blamed for the maid's unfortunate death."

James nodded. "Peculiar lot, the Froggies. Reckon Wellington'll rub their foreign noses in the mud for old England shortly though, eh?"

Sarah reached down to the groom who was waiting to help her dismount. As she stood on the newly washed cobbles of the yard she looked at Melissa again. The girl was staring at James Trefarrin, her face filled with ill-concealed malice mixed with a hint of fear.

Chapter Fourteen

The innkeeper seemed anxious to speak to Paul. "Mr. Ransome, before you partake of a meal, could I maybe have a word with you in private? It's rather important." He glanced surreptitiously at Melissa, who was still watching him.

Paul nodded. "Yes, of course, James. I came here to speak with you anyway. Melissa, if you and Miss Stratford will go on into the parlor."

He went off with Trefarrin, who began at once to speak in a low, hurried voice.

Sarah followed Melissa into the inn and soon the two women were sitting by a log fire sipping steaming mugs of mulled ale. Sarah did not like the taste, but the warmth was good. The flames leapt in the fireplace, sending sparks and smoke spiraling upwards. Copper pots and pans littered the stone grate, winking and reflecting the glow of the fire. A maid in a pale gray dress and white mobcap bustled around the cozy parlor, dusting and polishing the high-backed settles. In a far corner two men were deep in conversation over their ale, laughing occasionally and glancing surreptitiously at the two women who sat unattended.

The calm was disturbed suddenly and unexpectedly by Paul's furious voice in the passageway outside. Anger quivered in every muffled word and Sarah stared at the door, waiting. Melissa straightened slowly, sitting on the very edge of her seat. The door burst open and Paul stood there, his riding jacket buttoned and his

hat firmly on his head. He was pulling his gloves on
roughly and a shocked fury emanated from him. He
gazed reproachfully at his sister for a moment before
his anger reasserted itself.

Sarah stood, her heart beating swiftly. What had
happened? She saw James Trefarrin's anxious face behind Paul's shoulder, his watery eyes fixed on Melissa.

"Melissa, Miss Stratford, we return to Mannerby
immediately!" Paul's eyes were diamond bright.

"But why?" Sarah had to ask, for her curiosity
was great.

"My reasons shall be explained quickly enough.
Now please be so good as to do as you're told."

Sarah began to walk toward the door, tying her bonnet beneath her chin once more, but Melissa remained
where she was as if made of stone.

Paul's temper burst. "Melissa, get yourself up and
obey me, *now!* You especially are in no position to
defy me!"

Amazed, Sarah paused, for she had never before
heard him raise his voice to his sister. Melissa got to
her feet then and Sarah could see the naked fear on
her lovely face. As she walked past Trefarrin her eyes
were evil and he stepped aside quickly as if to avoid
all contact with her.

"Miss Stratford?" Paul spoke as patiently as he
could, but patience ran perilously low in him now.

In the yard the grooms were standing ready with
the horses. Sarah was lifted lightly into the saddle and
turned to watch as Melissa mounted too. Paul paused
for a last word with James Trefarrin, who was wringing his hands. "I'm sorry, sir, but I felt you had to
know what was going on."

"Yes, yes, you were right to tell me, James." Paul
was abrupt but his words seemed to satisfy the anxious
innkeeper, whose relief was obvious. He mopped his
brow with a large red handkerchief.

The ride back to Mannerby was swift and silent.
Melissa was tense, her face white and her lips pale,
and she looked increasingly apprehensive as each mile

passed. Sarah urged her mount along as best she could, finding the headlong pace difficult with the dreadful sidesaddle to contend with. She put all her concentration into remaining seated, and into ignoring the rumbling of her stomach which had now gone without both breakfast and lunch. Her body ached, she was tired, and she was bewildered. What on earth had the innkeeper revealed? It seemed to have been something concerning Melissa, that much was certain.

Already the short winter afternoon was drawing in and the sun had taken on a reddish hue so that the rocks on top of the tor seemed alight. Sarah saw with relief that Mannerby was in sight, for they were at last riding down the long incline toward the village. The villagers looked up in surprise as they saw the hurried return of the gentry from the big house. Martin had been painting the gates and he put down his brush, rubbing his hands on his leather apron. His keys jangled as he opened the gates.

Paul alighted almost before the Turk had stopped, turning to grab at the reins of Sarah's mount. "Sarah, go to your room if you please, and remain there." He reached up and helped her down and then turned to his white-faced sister. "Melissa, you will take yourself to the drawing room and await my coming."

Anger showed in his every movement as he helped Melissa to dismount. Sarah thought she heard a frightened little sob as the girl ran into the house, dashing past Marks, who stood aside in surprise.

"Go to your room, Sarah, please," Paul repeated. "I will come to explain as soon as I can." He met her glance and she saw that there was still a kind of stunned shock in his brown eyes.

"Is there anything I can do?" Surely she could help in some way.

He shook his head. "You can do nothing." He walked slowly and heavily into the house, taking off his hat and gloves and thrusting them into Marks's hands. As he vanished inside she suddenly realized that he had addressed her by her first name.

Sarah had not been in her room for long when a very excited Janie hurried in. "Miss Melissa's in awful trouble . . . awful."

Interest quickened in Sarah. "How do you know?"

"They're in the drawing room, her and Mr. Ransome, and he's shouting ever so loudly. I didn't think I'd ever hear him speak to her like that. She's weeping and wailing, and all the servants are in the hall trying to hear what's being said—even that miserable old Marks."

A door slammed and footsteps pattered up the stairs and along to Melissa's room. Another door slammed and there was silence.

Sarah waited, but nothing happened except for Melissa's maid putting her head around the door and telling Janie that Mr. Ransome wanted to see all the servants in the drawing room immediately.

Alone, Sarah went to her favorite seat by the window. A milkmaid was walking down the street with her yoke and two brimming pails of milk. From their small enclosure the three cows called after her, ears swivelling to and fro and mouths chewing steadily. Down in the courtyard she could see Martin's brush and pot of paint where he had left them when summoned to go and see Paul. The wintry sun was sinking in a blaze of crimson and gold and the tor was now a stark silhouette against the sky. The air was chilly and she closed the window, pausing only to glance at the dark line of the woods, her eyes seeking the horseman, although she did not consciously realize that she was looking for him.

Slowly footsteps climbed the stairs and approached her door. It was Paul, and she had opened the latch before he reached it. He looked inexpressibly tired and his eyes were empty as he went to sit by the fire.

"I don't know where to begin, Sarah, for I have discovered so much today which concerns you." She sat down in a chair facing him and he leaned forward. "Why didn't you tell me how cruelly Melissa was behaving toward you?"

She smiled. "Would you have believed me?"

Ruefully he returned the smile. "Perhaps not, perhaps not. Anyway, the truth is out now, for James Trefarrin after much deliberation decided to tell me. I am ashamed to say that my sister has been responsible for the spreading of all kinds of malicious gossip about you. Did *you* know that she was once engaged to your cousin, Edward Stratford?"

"Yes, I knew, but only by accident. I didn't know before I came here."

"Well, I found out only this very evening when I dragged from Melissa the reason for her behavior. She told me that she'd been about to marry Edward, then your father brought you to Rook House, telling Edward that he must marry you if he wanted to inherit anything. Is that true?"

She nodded, coloring a little. "Yes, it's true. It seems my father was determined at all costs to prevent Edward marrying the woman he loved. To this day I don't know why Melissa was considered so unsuitable. And before you think too badly of me for agreeing to this monstrous marriage, I wish to say that my life would otherwise be made intolerable. . . . At least with money there are compensations." She knew that she was coloring deeply now, but she felt the need to explain to him and was anxious lest he should think her totally grasping and only concerned with wealth.

He was silent for a while. "I can understand, Sarah, and there's no need for you to explain to me further, for I of all people have little right to any explanation from you. In my way I'm just as guilty as my sister of harming and hurting you, for I was willing enough to believe everything she told me." He reached out and took her hand gently. "Sarah, I don't wish to embarrass you, or alienate you, but must take that risk if I'm to tell you what Melissa has been doing. I think you should know."

She lowered her eyes, swallowing, wanting to know and yet afraid of what she would hear. "Then tell me."

"It began really when Melissa returned here last

autumn. Until then she had been living with our Aunt
Mathilda in London, enjoying the Season, going to
balls, and so on. I was surprised when she came back,
but she seemed unconcerned and so I did not press
the matter. When you were sent here it was a vile
stroke of luck for you, for Melissa's frustrations boiled
to the surface and she set about making your life un-
bearable and ripping your reputation to shreds." He
looked at Sarah across the dancing light from the fire.
"And she very nearly succeeded, didn't she?"

She looked away from him, glad of the darkening
shadows in the room. Outside it was dusk and the bell
in the church tower was echoing across the moor. She
could no longer see Hob's Tor, for the sun had faded
away behind the horizon, leaving no sign of its passing.

Paul released her hand and she turned back to him
quickly. "Sarah, I was ungentlemanly enough to mention a letter from Ralph once. Well, I must say here
and now that I've never even seen it. When I returned
here with you, Melissa told me that the letter had
arrived just after my departure and that she'd opened
it in case it contained some news which should be sent
on to me. It was merely, she said, a confirmation that
Ralph was expecting me to come to view his thoroughbred stallion. It also contained, so she said, an account
of Ralph's affair with you." He took her hand again
as she straightened, denial leaping to her lips. "I know
now that it was a lie, Sarah, for there was no letter
and Ralph never had a love affair with you." He held
her hand gently. "This affair with Ralph was supposed
to have been a torrid matter, and he professed himself
almost scorched by your fervor. He also was claimed
to have known that he wasn't alone in enjoying your
favors, for you were also engaged in dalliances with
several of your father's guests at Rook House. Your
name was becoming notorious, and your father an ob-
ject of ridicule because of your behavior. This infor-
mation is what greeted me on my return here to
Mannerby, and is partly why I found it so difficult
to—to . . ." His voice died on a note of the utmost

embarrassment as he remembered how coldly he had
behaved toward her.

"But you already disliked me even before we left
Rook House. I know that's so."

He was surprised, for he did not know that she had
overheard him that day on the grounds of Rook
House. "Well, I'll come to all that later, Sarah, for
I'm determined that you shall know all it's your right
to know." He ran his fingers through his sandy hair
and stood up, taking a candlestick from the nearby
table and holding out the candle to the flames of the
fire. Sarah watched the glow of the fire lighting his face.
He put the candle on the table and sat down again.
"Melissa was not content with that slander but had to
pursue her vendetta continuously. Using her maid,
whom I've now dismissed, she spread her vile tales
around the village, and even as far as Bencombe—which
at last proved her undoing. She had it said that you'd
been Jack Holland's mistress and that you'd set him
against Ralph Jameson merely for the pleasure of
seeing them fight over you. She said also that you'd
confided in her that you were not even truly Sir Peter's daughter, but an imposter out to gain all you
could." He hesitated briefly. "You were really, so
you're supposed to have revealed, a London whore.
Oh, my dearest Sarah, forgive me for saying all this."
He looked at her, his brown eyes pained.

"No, no, please tell me everything." Her voice was
small.

"There's not so very much more; just the matter of
the deaths of Armand and Betty. Melissa claimed that
you'd told her Betty was terrified of water and that it
had greatly amused you to send her across Hob's
Brook that day. That Betty's drowning had not concerned you, nor the fact that Armand had apparently
lost his life too for he 'was just a Frenchie and so
deserved to die like a rat.' They're gullible people and
they were bound to believe her, being the daughter
of the manor house." He was silent at last.

Sarah closed her eyes, shutting out the firelight and

the shadows, and also shutting out Paul's face as he gazed so intently and sadly at her. Now at last she knew, she understood why everyone in Mannerby so obviously disliked her. She knew too why that grotesque wreath had so offended everyone at Betty's funeral. Believing what they believed, it must have seemed an unbelievably callous thing to do, sending so extravagant a gesture of grief when they all knew what she was supposed to have done. She also knew why Martin was so determined that she should not have one of Kitty's puppies—she was too evil, too unspeakably bad. She opened her eyes and looked at Paul. "And how much of this did you know?"

"None, with the exception of what she claimed was in the letter. I knew, well, at least I sensed, that folk didn't like you, but I didn't give it much thought. Sarah, I've said and thought some very erroneous things, and all I can say is that I'm sorry—from the bottom of my heart, I'm sorry."

She could not think. "I must go away from here. I cannot stay now that I know what they all think—"

"They no longer think those things, Sarah. I've seen to that. I've had all the servants together and have told them precisely what Melissa has been doing. By the morning the whole village will be eager to put the matter right with you. They're good people, Sarah, only easily led, and they'll be horrified to know that they were so wrong—just as I'm horrified at myself. As for Melissa, well, she leaves Mannerby tonight. I've told Marks to have the coach prepared and her things are being packed right now. I'm sending her back to Aunt Mathilda in London, for her to deal with her as she thinks fit. You won't have to face my sister anymore."

"But would it not be better if I left tonight instead? After all, Mannerby is Melissa's home. I'm the stranger here."

"No, Sarah. Melissa has heaped disgrace upon my family and it's something I'll find hard to forgive. I'd have sent her away to my aunt even if you weren't here, so please don't think that the wrong person is leaving tonight. Melissa must go." He stood up and crossed the room to stare out of the window into the dark night. "There's more, you see, and my aunt is the one to deal with it. Melissa has a lover, a man she has been meeting on the moors. Those meetings were the reason for her frequent rides." He shook his head as if unable even now to believe he had been so gullible.

A thought struck Sarah. "Does he have a bright chestnut horse?"

He glanced around. "Yes. Why?"

"Oh, it's just that I've noticed a man on such a horse out there and he seemed intent on observing this house. He watches sometimes from the woods."

"Would you recognize him again?"

She shook her head. "No. I'd really only recognize his horse. It's a very distinctive animal, finely bred, very costly. As to the man, well, beyond the fact that he was most fashionably dressed, I couldn't say anything about him."

Paul was gazing out of the window again, past the slowly moving branches of the ash tree. "She met him at the Blue Fox once, and James came upon them unexpectedly. It was that which finally made him decide to tell me all the rumors which had been rife in the neighborhood, both about you and about my sister's meetings with her lover. They were very careful—Melissa probably feared that somehow Edward might hear of it and her chances of marrying him would be ruined forever."

"Perhaps it *is* Edward. After all he dresses in the height of fashion and—and he owns a horse like that." Sarah's eyes widened as she remembered the horse Edward had ridden to the hunt at Rook House.

Paul pursed his lips. "I wish it *was* Edward, but he's not even in England at present. Your father sent him away, probably to cool his ardor for Melissa. Edward has been attached to the Duke of Wellington's army for some weeks now. So whoever it is that Melissa has been meeting, it isn't Edward Stratford."

Sarah pondered. The man she had first seen with Melissa had looked like Armand, but the stranger on the bright red chestnut had been a taller man, better built, and very definitely dressed in the fashion.

Paul turned away from the window, looking thoughtful, and then at last he sat down and leaned toward her. "Sarah, I think perhaps I should confide in you some of the affairs of my family, for they touch upon your own family and I believe would explain my behavior a little."

She drew away, embarrassed. "There is no need to tell me such private things, Paul."

"But there is, there is."

"Very well, if you're sure you wish me to know."

"I am sure." The flame of the single candle sizzled and a droplet of molten wax coursed slowly down the stem, dripping to the base of the candlestick and solidifying. Sarah watched it intently as Paul began to speak. "Mannerby was my property until last autumn. I was the owner and not merely the tenant. A short while after my sister's return from London I received a letter from your father telling me that it would be in my interest to visit him immediately. I went, for the tone of his letter left me in no doubt that something serious lay behind it. He told me that he knew something about my sister which would ruin our name if it became public knowledge."

Sarah stared intently at the wax pool. How very like her father this sounded. She glanced at Paul then. "But what did he know? What was there to know?"

Paul lowered his eyes. "I did not ask him."

"You didn't ask him—? But why not?"

"Because I knew what he had discovered." Paul sighed and leaned back wearily in his chair. "There is something in my sister's past which even now I cannot bring myself to speak of. Suffice that it never comes out."

Sarah conquered the urge to reach out and comfort him. He looked so tired and shaken, and so very unhappy. Her hand dropped back. "Does it concern her nurse, Mother Kendal?" she asked quietly at last.

His eyes sharpened. "It is in the past."

"Forgive me."

"It's not that, please believe me. You are right, and some day I shall be able to talk of it, but not yet. It is done with, over and long since set aside. Except that your father somehow came upon it all. He had a price for his silence, and the price was Mannerby. He demanded that I sell him the house and neighboring lands for a price he fixed on. It was agreed that I should remain as tenant."

"But that's blackmail, Paul. He blackmailed you!"

'I know it. But there would be no such crime if humankind was not so frail and susceptible. I agreed to your father's price. I felt that I had no choice under the circumstances. He's a very ruthless man, and determined to acquire whatever he covets."

"I'm sorry, Paul, sorry that he is my father and that he did this to you."

He smiled thinly. "Oh, he came out of this excellently—he managed to break up the affair between his nephew and my sister, *and* he managed to acquire Mannerby into the bargain, a most admirable state of affairs as far as he was concerned. The land here does not amount to much. It was the stud he was after and the prestige ownership of it would bring."

Outside in the courtyard they heard the rattle of carriage wheels on the cobbles. The swaying light of carriage lamps slanted in through the window and Sarah stood up to look out. Martin was carefully opening the gates, trying not to touch the still sticky paint. Marks was supervising the loading of Melissa's trunks and baggage on to the coach, and from the stables Melissa's horse was led out and tethered to the rear of the coach.

She heard the door of the room close and looked around. Paul had gone. She waited by the window and soon saw his tall figure emerge with his sister. Melissa's emerald green skirts were silvery in the half-light and she clung to her brother's arm, but he removed her hand firmly. His every sense of right had been outraged and now he could hardly bear to be near her. Her head was bowed miserably as the door closed.

With a lurch the carriage moved away, out into the village street and away down the hillside. The whip cracked occasionally to bring the horses up to a good pace. Sarah watched until the darkness swallowed it.

Melissa was gone . . . and yet she felt no surge of gladness or triumph. Turning away from the window her glance fell upon the writing table where Janie had set out the paper, pen, and ink. She knew that she would never write that letter now.

Chapter Fifteen

Sarah could not face going downstairs again that night, but she had not eaten all day and felt sick with hunger. At last Janie suggested bringing a tray up to her room, and this she did. Sarah ate her solitary meal and then Janie drew the blue velvet curtains around her in the bed.

She lay there, sheltered and warm. But sleep was elusive and she watched the small movement of the curtains as a draft stole through them, tinkling the Buddha's head on its way. The dying fire glowed amber as it settled lower and lower in the grate, and the old house creaked occasionally, as if shifting in its own peculiar sleep.

Across the moorland the owls hooted, flying silently through the night with large, bright, all-seeing eyes. The wind whispered over the bracken and heather, murmuring its mournful little song as it eddied around the peaks. Mannerby slept, a lonely lantern swinging on the wall of the big house, casting its light over the shivering ivy leaves. The yew trees in the churchyard loomed black against the silvery light of the moon which rose now and sent a cool grayness over everything. Far away a dog barked, and Sarah lay there listening, wide awake.

The sound which disturbed the night was distant at first. Down in the gatehouse Kitty sat up, her ears pricked, a growl deep in her throat. The noise grew louder; it was a rattling, creaking, rumbling sound, and

Kitty's growl of warning became more intense. A whip cracked through the darkness and Kitty began to bark.

Martin sat up sleepily, rubbing his eyes and cursing as he fumbled to light a lamp. What was Kitty making all that noise for? Then his sharp ears heard the noise and he got quickly out of his narrow bed.

Upstairs, Sarah pulled aside the bed curtains and peered toward the window. What was happening? Kitty was barking her heart out! Janie crept into the room. "Oh, you're awake, miss. I came to see if the noise had disturbed you."

"I wasn't asleep, Janie. What is all the din? Do you know?"

"No, miss, but listen to it now! Just about every dog for miles is barking!"

They listened, and then suddenly Sarah recognized the sound which disturbed the slumber of the village. "It's a carriage, Janie, and driven at some speed too!" She climbed out of the bed and hurried to the window, pulling aside the curtains to look out.

Lights were flickering in several of the cottages now and down by the gatehouse Martin was pulling on his leather jerkin as he moved toward the gates to look out. Up the village street came the carriage drawn by four sweating horses. It was Paul's carriage, the one Melissa had left in earlier. The coachman reined in by the gates, shouting to Martin to open up. The coach swayed on its springs as the horses danced about, foaming and wide-eyed. The gates creaked in the dampness of the night air and the whip cracked as the coachman urged his tired horses into the courtyard. It was then Sarah noticed that Melissa's horse was missing.

Paul hurried out of the doorway as the straining horses clattered to a standstill. Sarah opened the window, shivering as the night air swirled in icily. The ash tree rustled its branches as if it sought to conceal the words of those down in the yard below.

"Mr. Ransome, she's gone. Miss Melissa's gone!" The coachman's voice was high with worry and fear.

"What do you mean, *gone?*" Paul seized the bridle of the lead horse to steady it.

"We failed to see a deep rut in the road, sir, and the carriage stuck fast, up to the boards. Jim and me, well, we had to both get down to see what could be done. It was more than we thought we could manage. Miss Melissa was in the coach then, for we heard her ask if she should remain where she was. Jim thought he heard horses coming along the road behind us and he went into the track with a lantern to hail whoever it was, for more hands would have done the trick, so they would."

"Yes, yes. Then what?" Paul spoke sharply and impatiently. Would the fool never get to the point?

"Well, they came closer, sir, close enough for us to see by the light of the lantern that one was riding a chestnut, a real bright red horse it was!" Sarah felt her heart begin to beat more swiftly and she leaned nearer to hear the coachman's voice, which had dropped a little. "Mr. Ransome, the man on the red horse stopped on the edge of the lantern light, and his companion behind him. We called to them, asking them to help, but they stayed where they were. Then the man we couldn't see called to Miss Melissa. 'Mamselle 'Lissa' he called her, and well, Jim and me we reckon it was that Froggie groom of hers. For he called her that."

"Armand!" Paul thumped his first on the side of the coach. "That crazy Frenchman seems to haunt me. And I thought he was dead!"

"Reckon we all did, Mr. Ransome, but it did sound like him. You know how he was with Miss Melissa, like a lapdog following her about. Maybe I couldn't swear on the Bible, but I'd go a long way toward that in saying it was him."

"And then what happened?"

"Well, she was out of the coach and on her horse before Jim and me really knew what was happening, and she almost rode us down. She and the strangers rode off together, going up toward the high moor. There was nothing we could do, sir. I'm sorry."

"When did this happen?"

"Over an hour ago. It took us all of that time to get the carriage free. We came back as quick as we could; drove like the devil I did. You could hear us coming for miles."

Paul's head was bowed. The patterned brocade of his dressing gown was a rainbow of subtle colors as he turned toward the butler shivering in his woolen coat. "Get everyone back to their beds, Marks. There's nothing can be done in the middle of the night." He nodded to the two coachmen. "Put the coach away and get yourselves to bed. It was not your fault and I put no blame on you."

"Thank you, sir."

"Martin, we'll make a search in the morning. Perhaps they left a trail you can follow."

Martin nodded grimly. "Aye, if they've crossed the moor I'll find their tracks, make no mistake."

Paul sighed. "Did you find out anything about this man with the red horse?"

"He's not from these parts, sir. I've been asking all over and there's not a soul knows him. Most reckon he's from London way, on account of the way he looks. As to it being Armand just now, well, I couldn't say about that. But this I do know: there's others have lost their lives in Hob's Brook but they've always been found in the end. The Frenchman's body was never recovered, and that's strange."

Paul looked up toward the distant moor and the dull gray silhoutte of Hob's Tor in the moonlight. "I thank God that Melissa knows her way."

Martin nodded. "The Green Pool, you mean, sir?"

Without answering, Paul went back into the house and Sarah drew back from the window. "Janie? What is the Green Pool?"

The maid shuddered. "It's a horrible place, miss, near the foot of Hob's Tor. A deep pool of water— bottomless some say it is—covered with green weeds and slime. It merges so well with the land around it that you can't see it's there at all. To someone who doesn't know, it's invisible. There's a few lives been lost up there."

They heard Paul walk past the door of the room on his way back to his bed, and Sarah felt heavyhearted. Such a lot had happened in so short a space of time.

She went back to the bed and climbed in, and soon Janie was returning to her slumbers too. For Sarah sleep was a world away and she lay there once more wide awake.

The moonlight outside faded as dawn approached. The wind died away and a mist rose from the land, hanging thickly in the valleys and sheltered spots, obscuring everything but the rocky summit of Hob's Tor which pierced the white blanket. With the vapor came that heavy silence which carries even the smallest sound for miles; but there was no sound.

The silence became overwhelming and Sarah sat up. Her eyes felt heavy with lack of sleep and her head was aching abominably. Perhaps some fresh air would clear it. She got out of the bed and went to her wardrobe, taking out her winter mantle and pulling on a pair of shoes. No one would see that she still wore her night robe. She went out of her room and down the stairs, past the Elizabethan lady and the huge Buddha, down the narrow staircase and past the tall grandfather clock which ticked its lonely way through the dawn.

The parlormaids were already about, hurrying to clean the fireplaces and to dust and polish everything before those upstairs arose. The butler remonstrated, "Miss Stratford, you should not go out at this hour."

She turned to look at him. "I'll be all right, Marks. I have such a headache that I think the fresh morning air will do me good. I couldn't sleep."

"I think everyone was awake last night, miss, especially the poor master." He came nearer, smiling as he opened the door for her. It was such a change to see friendliness in his eyes.

She nodded, and slipped out into the clammy mist. She pulled her mantle more closely around her and went down the steps on to the slippery cobbles. Lamps burned inside the gatehouse and as she walked across the courtyard she heard the whining of Kitty's puppies. The door was open and she stepped inside. Martin was putting down two dishes in front of the fire and the puppies waddled across to their breakfast, their little tails wagging.

"Good morning, miss. You're up early." Martin straightened, looking at her in surprise.

"Yes, I couldn't sleep."

"Nor I, miss, and it's going to be a hard day."

Nodding, she crouched down by the puppies, stroking their fat furry bodies.

"Would you like to hold one, miss?" Martin seemed anxious to please her.

"Oh, could I?" She held out her hands and he pushed a wriggling black-and-white puppy into them.

"That's Wellington, miss. You can have him if you want."

"He's not spoken for?" Her hazel eyes rested on his face.

"No, miss, and never was. I'm sorry for what I thought, miss."

She smiled. "It was not your fault, Martin, and anyway I'm delighted to make Wellington's acquaintance. What a funny name for a puppy."

"Well, they say there's going to be a great battle soon against the French, and that the Duke of Wellington will win it for England. So I thought that Kitty's first puppy should have as fine a name as I could think of—so Wellington it was."

Sarah cuddled the puppy in delight, smiling as the bright brown eyes looked up at her and the damp nose pushed against her hand. Kitty's head was on one side, tail wagging a little.

Martin stood up and pulled on his cap. "I must go now, miss, for I've a lot to do before we go to . . . to look for Miss Melissa."

Sarah put Wellington back with his brothers and sisters. "I must go too."

Martin semi-closed the gatehouse door behind them and then took out his keys and swung back the iron gates of the big house. He began to brush the cobbles, humming a little as he did so. Sarah hesitated and then stepped out into the village street, looking down toward the vague outline of the woods. The mist swathed everything with a gray monochrome which drained color away from all but the nearest objects. There were few villagers about this early, but already the cottages were lighted by morning lamps as the country people prepared for their long day. Opposite was the churchyard, and Sarah could see Betty's grave. She made up her mind to search for some wildflowers that day and put them on the grave. She had not been able to do that yet, apart from some snowdrops, but now it was March and surely there were some flowers to be found.

The drumming of hoofbeats carried through the mist and Sarah turned to look up the moor. Kitty came out of the courtyard and sat beside her, ears pricked with interest. Perhaps it was Melissa returning. Sarah walked a little way up the street, listening as the hoofbeats grew louder. Then suddenly the horses appeared from the depths of the mist.

Melissa's riderless horse came first, galloping at a headlong, frantic pace, and Sarah could feel the animal's terror as it approached. Behind it rode the stranger on the chestnut thoroughbred. Kitty began to bark again as Melissa's horse dashed past and into the courtyard. As it passed her, Sarah noticed the stain of green slime on its flanks.

The man reined in as he saw Sarah standing there. She could not see his face for he wore a high-collared cloak and a top hat which left his face in shadow. Growling and yapping alternately, Kitty ran forward, snapping fiercely around the capering hooves of the nervous horse. Sarah called to the dog but her voice went unheeded, for Kitty did not like this stranger.

The man's voice was gruff and angry as he tried to drive the little dog away. The horse's hooves began to scythe through the air as it reared and pranced. The man controlled it magnificently, but he could not save Kitty. The hooves cut into the soft black-and-white body and with a whimper Kitty fell to the ground.

Stunned, Sarah stared, feeling the eyes of the stranger resting on her for a moment before he gathered the reins and kicked his frightened mount away, back into the concealing mist.

Chapter Sixteen

Sarah was still standing there motionless when Martin darted past her. He bent to pick up the lifeless body of his beloved dog, speaking soothingly as if she could still hear him. Sarah closed her eyes as he carried Kitty back toward the gatehouse.

In the courtyard Melissa's horse was causing a good deal of commotion. Paul had been sent for and he arrived just as Sarah hurried back through the gates. He put his hand to the nervous, tired horse and patted it reassuringly, staring unhappily at the green stain on its coat.

Mark stood next to him. "That's from the Green Pool, sir. I'd know it anywhere."

Paul nodded. "Yes, but where in God's name is Melissa?"

"We could go to look now, sir. There's light enough and the mist will soon start to lift."

"Get everyone prepared then and have some food packed, for I've a notion we'll be out a long time." As he spoke, Paul saw for the first time the pitiful bundle in Martin's arms. "What happened, Martin?" he asked softly.

Martin could not speak—his throat was choked with grief—and Sarah stepped forward, putting her hand on his arm. "She was trampled to death, Paul, by that chestnut horse."

"When? Just now?" Paul's eyes flew to the gates and the street beyond.

"Yes, but he's gone now. He seemed to be pursuing Melissa's horse and stopped when he saw the animal reach Mannerby . . . and when he saw me watching him. Kitty was trampled beneath his horse's hooves, for she frightened it with her barking. The man headed back toward the moor."

Paul looked at her. "Melissa's horse returns, galloping as if for its life and covered with weed from the Green Pool, and chased by the man who was Melissa's lover? Why? Why chase a horse? What could have happened out there, Sarah?" He turned to look toward the ghostly outline of Hob's Tor which was now vaguely discernible through the grayness.

She stared in the same direction, wondering and unable to give him an answer.

It was late afternoon when at last the searchers returned. A small boy saw them first from his place on the high ground above the village where he tended a small flock of sheep. Forgetting his boots, he ran barefoot down the track, shouting and pointing. The village street soon filled with silent watchers as Paul Ransome returned.

From the doorway of the manor house Sarah looked toward the gateway, observing immediately how dejected he was and how grim his expression. The men with him looked equally severe, especially Martin, who still seemed almost dazed. Sarah shuddered.

Paul dismounted, unfastening his cloak and tossing it into Mark's hands. His eyes were dull as he glanced at Sarah's anxious face, then he shook his head slowly and walked past her into the house. He went straight to the drawing room and she followed him, watching as he took a decanter and poured himself a large glass of brandy. He drained the glass and immediately poured some more, loosening his cravat with stiff ringers and sitting down on a chair near the fire.

"She's dead, Sarah."

Her heart seemed to stop with the shock of what he had said. "You found her?"

Again he shook his head. "No, but we found the place where she died. We'll never find her body—that much I can tell you."

"Was it the Green Pool?" She pulled up a footstool and sat beside him.

"Yes, we found her cloak and gloves." He fumbled in his pocket and pulled out a pair of white kid gloves. His voice was trembling and he paused, breathing heavily to steady himself. "There were signs of a struggle, a terrible struggle. The hoofprints of her horse were everywhere to one side of the pool, large and slithering as if the animal had fought desperately to save itself falling in. Nearby were the smaller marks of 'Lissa's shoes, and those of a man's riding boots. The toes of the boots had dug deep into the soft ground as if he was pushing forward, forcing something or someone toward the pool. Then we saw the clawlike fingermarks in the mud as if someone had tried to clutch on to the firm ground. The green slime was disturbed close by, torn aside where someone had fallen through into the deep water beneath. It's a godless place, Sarah, and that's where Melissa lies." He choked.

She bit her lip, putting her hand on his wrist, her fingers crushing the thick white frills at his cuffs. What could she say?

He tore his arm away as he thumped his fist on the edge of the chair. "He murdered her, Sarah. I know it!"

"You must not think that!" She was horrified; murder was so terrible a crime. "It could be that you are reading all the signs wrongly and she is still alive."

He put down his glass and the lengthening shadows of the room seemed to swoop in as he leaned forward, cutting off the light from the fire. "Martin can read tracks as well as I can read a book. He looked very carefully at all the marks, seeing which was made first, and so on. The man, whoever he is, obviously meant to drown the horse as well, to make sure that there was no trace of my sister. He would have succeeded had it not been for the root of an ash tree which jutted out about a foot below the surface of the water. The horse gained a foothold which was just sufficient to give it the impetus it needed to drag itself clear. Even an animal has the intelligence to know when it's face-to-face with certain death. It broke away and made for the only place it knew—Mannerby. He had to give chase, for he knew that the green slime all over the horse would give us certain knowledge of where to come looking for Melissa. Fear must have lent wings to the animal for it to have outpaced his great stallion all that distance. He did not give up the chase until he realized that it was too late and it had reached a sanctuary. But for the escape of her horse, we would never have known."

"But, Paul, the very first place you thought of was the Green Pool. You would have looked there anyway, whether the horse had returned or not."

"Yes, that's true, but he would by then have destroyed all traces of what had happened. He intended to leave no trace at all. Melissa's body and that of the horse would sink without a trace. All he had to do was dispose of her cloak and gloves, then find a long stick to draw together the edges of the green weed, pulling it back into the place so that it covered the surface completely again. The prints in the mud could have been concealed with little trouble. Then he would have been safe, knowing that I would soon give up searching for her, thinking she had eloped with her lover. It would have been a perfect murder."

Sarah stared past him at the window. The setting sun glowed like a halo over the summit of Hob's Tor. "I wonder what happened? Why did he do it?"

Paul stood and poured himself another glass of brandy. "We'll probably never know. A quarrel most likely. . . . The quarrels of lovers can be devastating." He stood next to her, gazing out of the window too. "If the whispering rocks spoke a language I could understand, then they could tell what happened."

"The whispering rocks?"

With his glass he gestured toward the tor. "Out there, on the tip of Hob's Tor. Those rocks are called the whispering rocks because of the strange murmuring sound the wind makes around them. It's uncanny, just as if the rocks were talking quietly together. It's all superstitious nonsense really, but at times like this it's almost possible to believe in it."

"Why do you say they could tell you what happened to Melissa?"

"Because the Green Pool lies at the bottom of Hob's Tor; the rocks tower immediately over it. It's a quite horrible part of the moor really, and it has always been shunned by the local people. That's why James Trefarrin will have difficulty finding enough men to help him to go after that man who is stealing his sheep. No one wants to go anywhere near the place."

"Because of Mother Kendal and her coven?" Sarah broke in. "Oh, I've heard enough to guess the rest now, Paul. The nurse was teaching Melissa her craft, wasn't she? That's why your mother dismissed her."

He nodded slowly. "Mother Kendal practiced the black arts, Sarah, and Melissa helped her. I don't know what terrible things my sister may have done and I've no wish to know. She was at one time set upon an incredibly evil path under the influence of Mother Kendal . . . but we put a stop to all that. There's said to be a cave up there; Melissa told me of it once. I haven't seen it and I know of no one else who has, not even Martin, who knows every inch of the moor. No, the vagabond who is stealing sheep cannot be anyone who knows the reputation of the place or he wouldn't choose Hob's Tor to make his den."

Sarah stood. "Paul, perhaps he's the same man, the one with the red horse—"

He shook his head. "I'd thought of that, but the thief is a small fellow, thin and bony."

"Like Armand?" She looked at him.

He nodded slowly. "Yes, like Armand—and the Frenchman would have no fear of Hob's Tor for he was one of them."

"One of the coven?"

"Yes."

Sarah thought of the strange, intense eyes of the little Frenchman and she shivered. Yes, she could well imagine him practicing unholy magic.

There came a hurried knock at the door and Marks came in, his face at once both excited and anxious. "Mr. Ransome, sir!"

"Yes? What is it?" Paul turned, frowning.

"There's been a horse left behind the stable block, sir—"

"Well? Why bother me with such a trivial matter at a time like this?" He spoke sharply, irritated by such apparent foolishness.

"It's not just any horse, sir. It's a chestnut stallion, bright red and big, like the one—"

Paul left the room abruptly, and Sarah followed him.

The stable block was humming with interest, the lads standing in groups and the yard left unwashed for the moment. The Turk stood tethered to a rail, half groomed, a fact which would have infuriated Paul normally but which now passed unnoticed.

The double gate which led out on to the lower moor was open, and Martin stood there holding the reins of a great chestnut stallion. Sarah recognized it immediately.

It pricked its ears as Paul hurried over to it. It was truly a splendid creature, in its way every bit as fine as the Turk, and obviously very highly bred. Its coat shone and it had been groomed well, but the saddle was rough and functional, not seeming to match the style of the horse. There was nothing to identify either horse or rider.

Paul patted its neck, smiling at Sarah unexpectedly. "He's clever, this man. He knows that all we have to help identify him is his horse, and by leaving the animal on our very doorstep he's telling us that we'll never catch him and that it would be pointless even to try."

Sarah's hazel eyes moved from the arched neck of the horse to Paul's face, and she knew that he was right. "But James Trefarrin saw him. Could he not give a good description?"

"The description James gave could fit a thousand men, Sarah. Tall, well built, and dressed so fashionably as to be conspicuous on Dartmoor. But even with that we can find no trace of him." He patted the horse once more and turned away to go back to the house.

He stopped by Sarah. "He'll get away with it, you know. He'll go free even after murdering Melissa."

Chapter Seventeen

*N*othing was discovered during the ensuing weeks about the identity of the stranger who had been seen with Melissa. Paul's attempts to trace him through his horse led nowhere, and after a while there seemed little point in continuing. Melissa's lover would remain an enigma. And of Armand there was no trace; and no one ventured near Hob's Tor again.

For Sarah, life was strange without the oppressive presence of Paul's sister. She found herself half expecting the girl to walk in at any moment, or to come riding down from the moor as if nothing had ever happened. But Melissa did not come. And Sarah began to enjoy life at Mannerby, for she found the people so changed now. They were friendly, smiling at her often, and they were more than willing to pass the time of day in chat if she went for a walk outside the grounds of the big house. Even the vicar beamed at her, welcoming her to his church every Sunday and graciously bidding her farewell after each service.

Some months after Melissa's disappearance, news spread across England of a great English victory at a place called Waterloo. Napoleon had been vanquished and sent into exile, and England toasted her hero, the Duke of Wellington. Throughout July the land echoed and re-echoed to the sound of triumphant bells, pealing endlessly to celebrate the victory. In London preparations were made for festivities such as had never before been witnessed; and in Mannerby a puppy named Wellington sported a large white ribbon.

The news reached Mannerby only days after London had heard. A tired horseman spurred his horse along the road from Plymouth, shouting and waving his top hat before he had even reached the first cottage in the village. He told the news over and over again before digging his heels into his mount and galloping on to tell the news to Bencombe. The bell in the church tower rang for two days with few pauses, and Sarah laughed to see the vast quantities of ale which were carried to refresh the men who pulled so hard upon the ropes. A contest developed, for over the moor came the sound of Bencombe's bells, and it became a matter of honor that Mannerby's bells should peal for longer than their rivals. Paul sent out three bottles of his finest cognac when Mannerby was victorious.

After the initial furor and excitement, life settled back into its normal leisurely pace, but there was a jauntiness and air of cheer as a fierce national pride asserted itself firmly in every heart.

One warm, bright day Sarah took a walk in the kitchen garden. She wore a dainty gown of blue-and-white-striped silk, and Janie had labored for hours with the thick, black hair to produce a tolerable duster of Grecian curls. Sarah was determined to be cheerful on such a beautiful day, for she was at last coming to terms with herself. She knew that she meant nothing to Jack Holland and that she must forget him, since he had obviously forgotten her. It was a bitter pill, but one she must swallow. During the hours of daylight she succeeded in forgetting him; but at night, when she slept, he filled her dreams, and she sometimes awoke knowing that she had been crying. But today . . . today was not a day for thoughts of unrequited love. Sarah breathed deeply of the warm perfumed air, sniffing the fragrant herbs and the delicious smell of baking drifting from the kitchens.

The garden was springing to life. In the courtyard at the front of the house the tardy ash tree had at last unfurled its leaves, and its eager twigs were beginning to stretch out toward the window again. The lilac tree which grew in the shadow of the ash had blossomed profusely with pale, mauve-blue flowers, and from her room at night Sarah could smell the heavy sweet scent on the cool air.

From the kitchens came the sound of singing as two maids went about their tasks, and Sarah heard Marks's low voice shushing them from time to time—but to no avail, for they were soon singing again. It was that sort of day, lighthearted and determined to shake itself free of winter.

Sarah stopped in the shade of a tall poplar tree, glancing up as the breeze rustled the large, flapping leaves. The grass looked inviting and she sat down, putting out her hand toward a cluster of shriveled daffodil leaves, the flowers having long since disappeared.

"The daffodils were not at their best this year, I fear."

She looked up to see Paul standing there. He had just returned from exercising some of the horses and was dressed in his shabby working clothes. He wore no hat and his sandy hair was blown backward and forward by the breeze. He nodded at the flowers again. "This part of the garden is usually covered with them, but this year there were mostly leaves and very few flowers."

He watched her as she turned to look at the flowers again. The sun shone on her hair and the blue-and-white gown suited her well. She looked beautiful and carefree, but he remembered what Janie had confided to him. Janie was worried because her mistress cried in her sleep as if her heart was breaking, and occasionally called out the name of Jack Holland. Paul sighed. The man was not worthy of her, and never would be.

"Do you like flowers, Sarah?" He did not want to think further of her unspoken feelings for Holland.

"Oh, yes, I do. They remind me of my childhood."

She ran her fingers over the leaves, remembering how as a child she had walked barefoot through fields of daffodils.

"There is a stream near here which is always covered with irises, and it was as golden as ever last week when I rode past. Would you like to go there?" He felt awkward.

She stood eagerly. "I'd love to, Paul—really I would."

He smiled. "When would you like to go?"

"Now," she said firmly. "For it's a lovely day and perfect for such an outing."

He hesitated, taken aback. "But that's a little short notice. I have things to do—"

"Oh, Paul, work can surely wait an hour or two. Please take me now." Her hazel eyes looked up at him appealingly.

He could not refuse her. "I'll have the pony and trap made ready." He turned away and then looked back. "You're right. Work *can* wait for an hour or two. I shall tell Marks that we wish to take a picnic with us." He smiled, pleased with his decision, and then walked off whistling.

And so it was, an hour later, that a pony and trap set off at a spanking pace down the village street, skimming lightly along toward the woods. Sarah tied the pale pink ribbons of her flowery bonnet beneath her chin and sat back to enjoy the ride. The pony's mane flew in the breeze and its hooves clip-clopped loudly on the hard track. Through the woods they went, the hoofbeats muffled now by the thick green moss, and the sunlight dappled by the cobweb of branches overheard. There was no sign of the mysterious stranger who had been here those weeks before, and Sarah did not even give him a thought now.

The trap splashed across a tiny stream and set off down a narrow side track. The smell of the woods was strong and pricked Sarah's senses pleasantly. All around were the heavy white heads of hawthorn, their perfume sweet and fresh, and the pale faces of late windflowers lingered in the cool hollows. The trees were becoming more and more sparse and the track left the wood at last and wended its way through a small, quiet valley. High banks topped with hedges obscured the view until suddenly the banks fell away and Sarah could see the fields on either side.

Her lips parted with sudden delight, for there they were—the irises. They covered every inch of the meandering banks of the stream—tall, stately spikes of golden yellow among crisp green foliage. Paul turned the pony and trap through an open gateway and the wheels seemed to submerge in the tall grass.

He helped her down from the trap and began to untie the hamper of food. He spread a cloth upon the ground beneath a shady willow tree and sat back to watch Sarah beside the stream. She was lost in poignant memories of her childhood as she gathered an armful of the irises, burying her face in them.

Paul's voice startled her as he called. "Come on, or I'll forget that I'm a gentleman and will begin to eat without you!"

She walked back to him, and sat down, putting her huge bunch of flowers to one side and laughing as the cork of a wine bottle popped loudly. He grinned at her. "I thought that this feast should be washed down by the finest wine from the cellars—and we must not forget to toast the Duke of Wellington. It must be all of twelve hours since last we drank that noble gentleman's health!"

The wine was cool and a little dry, with a bite which was pleasing, especially with the wondrous fare the cook had packed away in the hamper. *I could remain here forever,* she thought as she leaned back against the willow tree, sipping the wine. She realized with a jolt that it had been some time since she had even thought of her father, of Rook House, or of her cousin Edward. Why had she heard nothing? After all, Melissa was dead and with her died the necessity for Sarah's marriage to Edward. She paused to consider this, for strangely the thought had not occurred to her before. She lowered her glass thoughtfully, a coldness in the pit of her stomach. Why had she not heard from her father? Did he intend to leave her on Paul's hands and conveniently forget all about her now that she was no longer of any use to him?

Embarrassment colored her face hotly and she glanced at Paul. Surely the same thought must have crossed his mind.

He felt her eyes on him and looked up, seeing the change in her. "What is it?"

"I—I was wondering why I've heard nothing from my father."

"He no doubt has his reasons—most probably devious ones at that."

"Yes, but, Paul, there's no reason for my marriage with Edward now that, now that . . ." She could not mention Melissa. "I've no illusions about my father and fear that he no longer wants me."

He sat up. "That's nonsense, Sarah, and you mustn't think such things. Of course he wants you. Anyway"—he smiled—"there's always a place for you at Mannerby."

She returned the smile. "I don't think that that would be seemly, Paul. I've been thinking about it. The situation is rather, er, lacking in propriety."

He leaned back again. "I'd already thought of that and so have written to Aunt Mathilda in London. She's a veritable termagant and led my poor uncle a merry dance during his lifetime, but she will make an excellent chaperone for you. She replied to my letter, saying that she will come, but I must say that her tone was curt in the extreme. I have a feeling that she is displeased with me for some reason. Still, that matters nothing, for I vow that no one would dare to believe any ill of our conduct while we're under her eagle eye. I still find it hard to believe that Melissa managed to conduct her affair with Edward while living under my aunt's roof."

Sarah felt a little apprehensive about being put in the charge of the formidable Aunt Mathilda. She took a slice of the cook's excellent cake and ate it slowly, staring dreamily over the scene before her. This moment could go on forever, she decided.

Paul sat up and looked at his fob-watch. "We must go shortly, for my work cannot wait any longer. Oh, I almost forgot—we're invited to the Blue Fox tomorrow, for dinner. A victory feast, James called it, to celebrate Waterloo! Would you like to go?"

"Yes, I would."

"Then that's settled. Come on now. We must go back."

"You're a fearful taskmaster, Paul, but just this once I'll forgive you." She smiled at him.

He paused as he put the glasses back into the hamper, watching her as she gathered her irises. Perhaps it was just as well that Aunt Mathilda was coming, he thought, for Sarah was tantalizingly lovely and he found himself enjoying her company far too much.

The whip cracked as the pony and trap rattled back toward Mannerby. The pony's ears pricked as it neared home, and its legs seemed to fly through the air. They clattered through the open ironwork gates into the courtyard, Sarah laughing and holding her bonnet tightly onto her head.

The pony shied at the bright yellow phaeton with its scarlet wheels. Sarah stared at it, and Paul cursed as he brought the dancing pony under control again.

And then she saw him. He stood in the doorway, his copper hair as unruly as ever, his elegant body clothed to sartorial perfection.

As Jack Holland smiled at her, the air seemed to sing.

Chapter Eighteen

She could feel a sudden breathlessness as she looked at him. He was just as her memory painted him, from the lazy way he walked down the steps toward her, to the roguish light in his gray eyes as he reached up to lift her down from the trap.

The irises spilled from her lap as she slid down, her blue-and-white skirts hissing.

"You're as lovely as ever, sweet Sarah." Even his voice, each slight inflection, seemed a soothing balm to her. This was what she had longed for, what she had forced out of her mind; until now. . . . How could she have thought she was over her love for him? How could she have even thought it was possible to forget him, when every sense swam so giddily at his being so near and her lips could not help their foolish smiling. He was all that mattered, all that had ever mattered . . . and now he was here.

"It's been a long time," she said, knowing that the words sounded lame.

The harness of the pony and trap jingled as Paul climbed down, handing the reins to Martin. "What brings you to Mannerby, Holland?" There was a definite coolness in his voice and Sarah was instantly aware of it.

Jack looked away from her. "I come on Stratford's business, Ransome. It's a small matter concerning the stud." He was smiling, but his eyes were half closed, as if to conceal their true feelings, and there was a thinly disguised contempt in his bearing which Paul could not help but notice.

Sarah glanced from one to the other in surprise. What had these two to dislike in each other?

Paul inclined his head stiffly. "Then no doubt you'll seek me out directly." Nodding briefly at Sarah he turned on his heel and went toward the stable block.

There was an expression of challenge in Jack's eyes as he watched the other man walk away, for all the world as if some unseen gauntlet had been thrown down. He looked at Sarah again, his eyes softening and his smile becoming as warm as the spring day itself. He took her hands and pulled her to face him properly. "My sweet, sweet Sarah, I have missed you."

The directness of his approach covered her with confusion. It was what she so wished to hear him say, and yet when he did so she was thrown completely off balance. She became uncomfortably aware of the curious glances of the groom who was leading Jack's yellow phaeton toward the stables, and of Marks who stood inside the doorway waiting for her.

"If you've missed me, why did you not come to see me sooner?" She was angry with herself immediately the words had passed her lips. Why could she not be satisfied that he had come at all instead of carping at the delay? After all, she had no right to expect anything of him, anything at all.

His thumbs caressed her palms. "I came at the first suitable moment, Sarah. I had to have a good reason for calling here at Mannerby or the gossipmongers would begin their chattering again."

She raised her eyes to his face, trying to hide her longing but not succeeding. "And now you have a good reason?"

He released her hands and walked slowly toward the lilac tree. She walked at his side. The lilac filled the air with its sweetness as he ducked his head beneath a low branch. "Yes, I have a perfectly legitimate reason for coming, and I have the Duke of Wellington to thank."

"The Duke?"

"Yes. Had he lost Waterloo then I would still be casting around for my reason. Napoleon's defeat meant that your father could realize a cherished ambition. There is a stud in France, a very fine one, on which your father has cast his covetous eyes this longtime. Now it is his. He paid a goodly sum for it, I might add, and I was instrumental in achieving all this for him. Your father has a great admiration for French horseflesh, whereas Ransome holds a poor view of both the French and their horses. I am here to, er, pave the way, you might say, because Ransome has to be informed that the French horses will be replacing some of his stock here. He will not take it kindly."

"You? *You* are doing all this for my father? That will surely cause no small ripple in London's best circles."

He smiled lazily. "I'm a law unto myself, Sarah. Had you not realized that yet?"

She thought of Ralph Jameson. Yes, Jack was indeed a law unto himself. "But what of Paul? There's nothing wrong at all with the way he conducts Mannerby." She knew she was defending Paul.

Jack's eyes were opaque. "You rush to protect him." He spoke quietly.

"Why yes, and why should I not? The results of his hard work and care are there for all to see. Mannerby horses are the finest in England. There can be little justification for what my father seeks to do."

"Your father owns Mannerby and is perfectly entitled to do as he pleases. Besides, I was not and am not concerned with the rights and wrongs of what is proposed. . . . It's merely a means to an end for me."

"I wish there was some other way." She glanced toward the stables.

Jack raised an eyebrow. "I begin to envy Ransome having such a spitfire to defend him. Perhaps I've left it too late to come here."

She was startled. "Oh no, it's nothing like that, please believe me."

"I find it a little disconcerting that you should strive so in his defense, Sarah. Perhaps these weeks here without a chaperone to watch over you have not been wasted by the redoubtable Mr. Ransome."

She colored. "That was not necessary, Jack."

"He was lacking in common sense, Sarah, for he should have seen to it that you were not alone in the house after his sister's death."

"Oh, you know about Melissa then?"

"It was in the London papers. She was of some interest, being the sister of Paul Ransome. As you say, the Mannerby stud has an enviable reputation." He reached up and snapped off a twig of lilac, twisting it between his fingers until the blossoms spun.

"Jack, Paul was not lacking in common sense. He has sent for a relative to come here, and, besides, what else could I do but remain here? I have nowhere else to go and my father has ignored me since I left Rook House. Perhaps he is too occupied with Liza." It was unfair to drag Liza's name in, but Sarah could not help it. She felt unhappy and insecure, more insecure than her father's unloved little mistress.

"Liza? Oh yes, my late wife's maid and now your father's, er, companion. No, I don't think poor Liza fills his thoughts very much. And you're wrong about your father, Sarah. He has not ignored you. He's one of those men who doesn't put pen to paper unless he has something specific to say. He will write to you when he wishes you to return to him, not a moment before. The only news I can give you is that the preparations are apparently going ahead for your marriage to Edward, and that your father has at last succeeded in engaging the services of a lady to instruct you. You see, I made it my business to find out all I could."

Her heart sank. So there was to be no change in her father's plans then. Melissa's death made no difference. "Oh. I had thought—"

"What?" He saw the despondency steal over her face.

"I had hoped that the marriage would be dropped now that Melissa is dead."

"Melissa? What has the late lamented Melissa Ransome to do with it?"

"She was the woman Edward had fallen in love with."

"Ah." He handed her the sprig of lilac. "She was very beautiful by all accounts—I didn't know her, but have heard it said." He leaned back against the trunk of the tree. "It cannot have pleased her to have you here."

Sarah remembered the hate which had filled Paul's sister and she shivered. "No, it didn't please her at all."

"Well, I'm afraid that the idea of you marrying Edward still appears to rather appeal to your father. He wants to keep his family fortune intact. Melissa makes no difference; you are doomed to make an unhappy marriage." The gray eyes wavered away from her face and she found herself wondering about his marriage—about his wife. What had really happened to her?

He held out his hands. "Come here, Sarah." She went to him and he kissed her. That kiss left her still deeper in his spell. She returned the embrace, forgetting all else but her great love for him.

He untied her bonnet and hung it on a branch of the ash tree. It swung there in the breeze like an immense flower, its long pale pink ribbons streaming and flapping. He rested his cheek against the softness of her hair. "Well, at least we may look forward to a week or so together."

Somehow she felt a vague, barely tangible disappointment. He made no protestations of love. He did not speak of persuading her father to change his mind. He did not mention wanting her himself. She swallowed. "You will be here for that long, then?"

"Until the French horses arrive. Ransome will have to put up with my company, I fear."

"Why don't you like him?"

"For the same reason he doesn't like me."

"And what reason is that?" She looked up into his eyes.

He smiled slowly. "I rather fancy we both desire the same woman."

Desire? But that was not the same thing as love. She looked away, knowing that she was blushing. "I think you are wrong. Paul regards me merely as a friend, no more."

"You don't do yourself justice, Sarah. I saw the look on his face when you first drove into the courtyard. . . . He regards you as something more than a friend."

Desperately she turned away, biting her lip. "And how do you feel about me, Jack?"

He put his hands on her shoulders and turned her to face him. "Do you need to ask?"

"Yes—yes I do. What *do* you feel?"

"Oh, Sarah, I thought you could see it written on my face. I love you. Of course I love you. I've had a wife; I've had mistresses, but you are the one I have fallen in love with. I hardly know you and yet I feel that you've always been there."

She closed her eyes weakly. He loved her; he said that he loved her.

Someone coughed apologetically and she turned, covered with confusion, to see Marks standing there. "I'm sorry to interrupt, madam, but it's about the meal. The cook is threatening all manner of things if it's not eaten soon, for it will spoil. Mr. Ransome says that he will not be eating, and so I was wondering if you and . . ." He glanced at Jack.

Sarah cleared her throat, her head still spinning a little. "Of course, Marks, we'll dine now. Please present my apologies to the cook."

As Jack took her hand to walk into the house she could have danced. She could have laughed and sung, so great was her joy. He loved her. Jack loved her. . . .

Chapter Nineteen

*I*t soon became apparent that the changes Sir Peter intended at Mannerby were swinging. In the morning after Jack's arrival, the two men were closeted together in Paul's study for two hours, and Sarah, sitting in the drawing room next door, could not help but overhear some of what was said. She sat quietly with a book upon her knee, and the same unread page faced her for a long time. She gleaned from the fragments of conversation which drifted to her that her father was going to change most of the stock, and then put in another man, of his own choosing, to run the stud with Paul.

Her heart was heavy when at last she rang the bell for Marks to bring some refreshment for them all. Sadly she turned the unread page of her book. There was little if anything to fault in Paul's management of the stud, and yet her father must change everything; to Sarah it seemed like change for the sake of change, little more, and knowing as she did that her father's method of gaining Mannerby had been underhand, she found herself almost despising the absent Sir Peter. It was the beginning of the end for Paul. Her father intended to oust him completely; Sarah could sense it. Through the open window she saw Martin carefully washing and polishing the yellow phaeton, and she thought of Jack. She knew why he had come, why he had chosen to lower himself by conducting her father's business, but she did wish that he gave at least the semblance of regret at what he was doing to Paul Ransome. But Jack seemed to find no difficulty at all in telling Paul that his life's work at Mannerby was to be wrecked.

Marks entered with a silver tray holding gold-and-white cups and saucers, a dish of the cook's fine spice biscuits, and a tall silver coffee pot. As he set it down beside her she suddenly remembered that she and Paul had been invited to the Blue Fox that evening.

"Has Mr. Ransome made any mention of today's evening meal, Marks?"

"Yes, madam. At least he did so yesterday morning. He said that the staff could all have the afternoon off as you and he would be dining out." He went to tap on the door to the study.

"Thank you, Marks," she said, as he walked slowly from the room and closed the door behind him. Did the invitation now extend to Jack? she wondered. She and Paul could hardly go without him, for that would be the height of bad manners.

Chairs scraped in the adjoining room and Paul and Jack came out. She met Paul's gaze for a moment and then lowered her eyes uncomfortably. Yesterday's picnic might as well have been enjoyed by two strangers, for there was more of a barrier between them now than ever there had been during Melissa's life.

Jack sat down beside her, his hand clasping hers in the folds of her peach-colored morning gown. "We have sadly neglected you this morning, Sarah, but now we are come to foist our company upon you once more." He lifted her hand to his lips and kissed it.

Paul looked decidedly bored and stretched his long legs out before him as he lounged in a crimson velvet chair. Sarah was aware of the studied manner in which he did this and she was a little piqued. It hurt her that he should turn so swiftly and so coldly away from her like this. After all, he must have known that she loved Jack, so why should Jack's actual presence make any difference?

Marks returned and stood by Paul. "I've come to

remind you of your words yesterday, sir. At what time may the staff take their afternoon off?"

Paul looked startled and had quite obviously forgotten. "Oh yes, it had slipped my mind." He glanced at Sarah. "We're invited to the Blue Fox, aren't we?" A brief smile touched his lips and then was gone, leaving her almost in doubt as to its ever having been there.

"Yes, Paul, we are, but if you'd rather not—"

"No. My word has been given, both to the staff here and to James Trefarrin." He stood, obviously wishing that he did not have to utter the next words. "Holland, of course, the invitation now extends to you as well, for you are my guest here."

Jack's gray eyes were impenetrable. "Thank you, but no. I'm sure that Mr. Trefarrin has no wish to entertain me, a stranger. I won't embarrass him—or you. Perhaps Marks here could arrange for a cold supper to be left for me. I will go for a ride on the moor instead."

Sarah was disappointed. She did not wish to be parted from him, even for so short a while, but she knew that he was only doing what etiquette demanded.

Paul nodded. "Very well. Marks, will you see to that for me? And you may all leave directly after the midday meal has been served."

"Yes, sir. Thank you, sir." Marks left silently, and Sarah realized that she hardly ever heard the old butler either coming or going.

Paul took the cup of coffee she held out to him, not looking at her but at Jack. "When do these French beasts arrive, then?"

"Sometime within the next few weeks. They're to be shipped to Plymouth and word will be sent to me directly they arrive." He smiled but his eyes remained cool. "You look as if you regret the outcome of Waterloo, Ransome. Such thoughts are treasonable."

Paul put down his cup quietly. "I'll be proved right in the end. Sir Peter is an atrocious judge of horseflesh."

Jack's smile did not waver. "But *I* have picked these animals, Ransome."

Paul stood, smiling with equal falsity. "Stratford must be unable to believe his luck in having so exalted a stable boy." Still smiling, he took his leave of Sarah and went out.

Jack laughed as the door closed behind him. "There's fire in our friend—not a great deal, but nonetheless, it is there."

She said nothing, knowing how deeply Paul was feeling the situation. She could not understand Jack, or indeed any man, she decided—and men had the audacity to say that women were unpredictable!

Later, after all the servants had gone for the afternoon, Sarah sat in the kitchen garden. Jack had gone for his ride on the moor and Paul was busy in the stables with a mare who was having difficulty giving birth to her first foal.

She looked up at the flawless blue sky. The day was warm, so warm. . . . In the stableyard she could hear the horses being led out for their afternoon gallop on the lower moor. Their hooves clattered noisily on the cobbles. From the farrier's shed came the acrid smell of smoke and the sound of a hammer on the anvil.

She unfastened the top two buttons of her high-throated gown, wishing now that she had worn the blue-and-white silk instead. Beyond the garden the moor shimmered in the heat. The leaves of the heather were fresh and green and the birch trees which lined the route of a stream were a ribbon of pale green and silver. The gorse which littered the moor was alight with bright golden flowers and as she looked away into the distance, Hob's Tor seemed to sway in the haze. There was no mist or cloud to engulf it today and she could see clearly the great boulders on its summit, those whispering rocks of which Paul had spoken. She wondered what their whispering sounded like. She was so lost in her thoughts that she did not see the dog cart coming down the track from Bencombe. It came into the courtyard and through to the stableyard, its driver calling for Paul.

She yawned and leaned back against the tree, wishing that she was out riding with Jack. There was a heaviness about the afternoon which made her drowsy, like some powerful opiate which was determined to deaden her every sense.

Paul's boots were almost silent as he crossed the grass to where she sat by the poplar tree. He sat down beside her, touching her arm to draw her wandering attention. "So sleepy, Sarah?" There was a hint of his former friendliness in the smile he gave her.

"I'm ashamed to admit it, but I am sleepy. It's so hot I think I'll change my gown for one a little cooler."

"There'll be thunder before midnight, Martin informs me, and he's seldom wrong."

"But we shall be back from Bencombe long before that, surely?"

"Well, that's what I've come to speak to you about. I'm afraid that we'll all be eating cold suppers tonight, for news has just come from James that there was a fire at the Blue Fox this morning and some damage done. He cannot entertain us tonight, nor for some time I fear."

"How terrible. Was anyone hurt?"

"No. The parlor has been destroyed and part of the kitchens. Anyway, I'm going to ride over to see if there's anything I can do to help." He stood up, brushing the grass from his breeches.

"Paul, how is the mare in foal?"

"She is well enough, the mother of a sturdy son!" He smiled, and then crouched down beside her again, his face serious. "Sarah, do you love Holland?" He spoke softly.

"Yes, I have since I—almost since I first met him."

He took her hand, "Then be careful. Don't do anything you may later regret."

A blush swept hotly over her and she snatched her hand away. "I think I may be trusted to behave myself, thank you!"

He stood once more, nodding. "I meant no insult, Sarah. I only sought to—to . . ." He shrugged and turned away, swinging his riding crop to slice at the leaves of the poplar tree. She watched him until he was out of sight.

She stood up, still feeling the hot flush on her face as she walked back toward the house to change her gown. As she reached the doorway she heard Jack's voice and turned. He was standing by the gatehouse where Martin was inspecting the foreleg of his horse. He saw her and crossed the courtyard toward her.

"What's happened to your horse?" she asked.

"I hadn't long gone when it went lame. I walked back with it. I hear that your visit to the Blue Fox has been canceled."

"Yes, there was a fire there this morning."

He took her hands and her anger at Paul was dispelled immediately. It would be deliciously wicked to contemplate misbehaving with Jack. . . .

Loosening his excellent cravat, Jack smiled. "Then shall we take fresh mounts and ride together?"

Her eyes brightened. That would be marvelous. "I would love to, except—"

"Except what?"

"Well, I don't think Paul would appreciate such an unescorted ride."

His eyes clouded with anger and he thumped the trunk of the ash tree beneath which they now stood. "And why should his objections carry any weight?"

"Because I am placed under his protection. Jack, I dare not flout his wishes. It would not be right."

"No, but it's perfectly acceptable for you to go picking flowers alone with him?" There was an edge to his voice.

She slipped her arms around his neck and leaned against him, ignoring Martin's interested gaze. "I'm not in love with Paul—there is the difference."

His arms tightened around her immediately and he held her close. "Then how can we manage our ride? There must be some way." His lips were against her hair and a shiver of delight ran through her.

"Janie and Martin," she said, catching sight of Martin. "They could come with us."

Jack laughed. "But surely they too would rather be alone? They are 'courting strong,' or so I believe."

"Yes, but Janie's mother is very strict. I think they would welcome the chance of riding with us, and then we can all chaperone each other and all impropriety will be eliminated." She smiled up at him and he kissed her again. She could hear nothing but the thundering of her pulse and she knew that Paul's warning had been justified; her love for Jack passed common sense and verged on the willful. Why, oh why, could her future not be with him instead of Edward?

A short while later she and Janie were in the kitchens rifling the cook's cupboards and shelves. It was like playing truant, thought Sarah, as she packed a warm loaf into the hamper.

The sun was still high in the sky as the four rode up the village street toward the moor. Janie and Martin rode side by side, chattering together cheerfully, the hamper bumping against the shoulder of Martin's sturdy horse.

Before them spread the glittering, sun-drenched moor, crowned by the pinnacle of Hob's Tor.

Chapter Twenty

A n ancient bridge of stone crossed a wide stream which babbled lazily over pebbles, splashing and sparkling in the sun. The horses paused by the water, dipping their muzzles into the cool stream.

Sarah breathed in deeply the mixed smells of the wild countryside. Bracken, heather, foxgloves, and moss all intermingled with the perfume of gorse; combined they made Dartmoor. Hob's Tor seemed unexpectedly near as she looked at it. Each boulder on its rocky tip could be discerned and the heat made the hill dance. It seemed to be trying to attract her attention, she thought, immediately shaking her head at such a foolish notion.

"What hill is that?" Jack pointed with his crop.

Martin looked at it. " 'Tis Hob's Tor, sir."

"*Hob's* Tor? Is it a place of magic then?" Jack was grinning.

Martin looked back at him seriously. "They say it's a place where the hobgoblins go, sir. I wouldn't know about that, but one thing is certain: it's an evil place. Things used to happen there, bad things."

Jack was interested. "What sort of things?"

"Well, I can't say for certain, sir, but things to do with witchcraft—you know, sir, the Old Religion. 'Tis not so long since the Old Religion was followed hereabouts. At certain times of the year they made sacrifices on Hob's Tor. And other things were done. . . .

Anyway, the place has a bad name now, and no one will go there unless they have to."

"What a lot of nonsense. It's only a hill like any other hill. It doesn't look far—shall we ride there and prove everyone wrong?" Jack turned his horse and looked toward the tor.

Janie looked dismayed. "I'd rather not, sir, please."

"Sarah?"

Sarah stared at the tor, feeling its curious mute beckoning and the strange appeal of the whispering rocks. She felt suddenly that she must go there. She glanced at Janie and Martin. "Oh come on, you two. It cannot harm us to go there. Perhaps we can have our picnic somewhere on its slopes."

Jack waited no longer; he spurred his horse forward through the stream, ignoring the bridge. The water sprayed up in shining droplets which spattered over Sarah as she followed him. Very reluctantly, Janie and Martin rode across the stream and toward Hob's Tor.

The heat played them false for the tor was further than it seemed and it was fully two hours before they reached the lower slopes. Sarah was hot and thirsty, but still determined to have the picnic on the tor. No one had noticed that the sun had become less intense. The shadows of their horses were blurred now and not sharply defined as they had been. From behind them came spreading across the skies an angry bank of yellow storm clouds. The blue of the sky was turned to gray.

Unexpectedly the land sloped downwards before them to a small, deep valley which could not be seen from further away. Sarah reined in abruptly, for an unpleasant sensation was moving over her, tingling across her scalp and resting coldly on her damp skin. Jack glanced at her in surprise. "What is it?"

"I don't know." She spoke truthfully. Something about that little valley disturbed her. Beads of perspiration stood out on her forehead as she stared down into the grassy hollow; but there was nothing there, nothing which could cause her such alarm.

Martin moved his horse alongside. "Miss Melissa drowned down there." He pointed into the valley.

Sarah held her breath, almost overcome by the malevolent sensation which swept over her in wave after wave of revulsion. *Melissa.*

Jack looked down into the hollow. "It's hard to credit that anyone could drown in there. You can't see a trace of the pool."

"Aye, but it's there right enough." Martin spoke in a hushed voice, almost as if someone or something might hear him.

Jack nodded. "Between those two rocks, isn't it?"

Surprised, Martin glanced at him, filled with a new respect for the townsman whose keen eyesight could see the almost invisible. "That's right, sir. It's bounded on the far side by that broken tree and on this side by the gorse bush."

Jack gathered his reins. "Well, I see that the tree is an ash, so I begin almost to believe your tales of witchcraft and sacrifice, Martin. Come on or it will be dark before we even begin to eat." His horse began to descend, stones crunching and rattling beneath its hooves. As she followed him, Sarah felt as if she was descending into the pit of hell. She could almost hear the wild fluttering of her fear as they went lower and lower toward the floor of the valley. High above loomed Hob's Tor, towering and immense now they were so close. She wished that she had sided with Martin and Janie, for everything about this place was horrible.

The valley was silent. No birds seemed to frequent it and none of the small moorland creatures scuttered before the horses as they had done before. It was as if nature shunned such a place. Even the flowers were subdued, hardly moving their bowed heads in the breeze which was picking up as the storm overhead mushroomed across the heavens. But the breeze seemed to avoid the bottom of the valley, for everything was still and breathless there, not a blade of grass moved.

Sarah stared at the motionless expanse of green before them. Not a ripple showed the presence of that evil pool; the green was flawless, solid-looking, and infinitely deceitful. Was Melissa there? Was she? Sarah glanced warily at the broken ash tree—only an ash tree would grow in such a place, she thought.

The horses were uneasy, moving forward unwillingly. They knew, thought Sarah, sinking further into the realm of superstition; the animals knew. . . . This valley was bad.

"Well, one thing is certain: we cannot ride up there." Jack was looking up the steep slope of the tor. "We'll have to eat here."

"Eat here? I couldn't." Sarah's eyes were huge.

"Nor I." Janie swallowed, edging her horse closer to Martin's.

Martin sighed reluctantly. "I don't like the place but I must agree with Mr. Holland. We cannot go any further without eating. Besides . . ."—he indicated the gathering storm—"the storm's coming quicker than I thought and we'll have to get to some sort of shelter before long."

They dismounted, tethering the horses to the gorse bush whose golden flowers were somehow duller than its fellows on the open moor. Sarah looked at the flowers and was not surprised; she felt, like the gorse, drained of sparkle and vitality, as if the pool was sucking everything from her.

Silently they ate, with only Jack showing any great appetite. He poured himself a glass of wine and then stood up, wandering a little way up the tor amongst the huge rocks and boulders which littered the ground. A vague rumble of thunder in the distance gave the first hint that the storm was almost over Dartmoor. Martin glanced up at the yellow-gray clouds which billowed angrily high above.

"We'll not get to shelter, I fear, so we'd best resign ourselves to getting wet." As if it heard him, the storm released the first heavy raindrops. Janie hurried to pack away the food in the hamper and Sarah helped her.

Jack shouted suddenly, "There's a cave here, with shelter enough for us till the storm's over." He hurried down the slope, scattering dust and pebbles before him. "Make the horses fast and then we can get inside before the rain really comes down."

The wind picked up with a warm gust, lifting Sarah's light skirts and bringing with it the smell of the moor surrounding this awful valley. She stared toward the hidden cave. Mother Kendal's cave. She felt cold and sick. A slow, insidious hissing sound spread over the little valley and Sarah's heart seemed to tighten in her breast.

"Listen." She held up her hand and the others fell silent as a new sound filled the air.

They could all hear it. A stealthy murmuring, whispering sound as if there was some hidden enemy nearby. The sound moved around the valley, seeming to come from every direction at once. Goose-pimples prickled all over Sarah's body and something akin to terror rushed over her. The horrible, unintelligible whispering grew louder and she bit her lip to hold back the whimper which trembled near.

"It's the whispering rocks." Martin's voice came as a surprise. It was so ordinary and normal after the unearthly rustling of that other sound.

"No wonder everyone stays away from here." With wide eyes Sarah stared around the valley, and she would not have been surprised at anything just then. Every primeval instinct was aroused, every sense and fiber quivering with fear.

Jack saw her alarm and took her hand firmly. "Come on, let's get to that cave."

The rain was pattering on the dry earth as they passed the edge of the hidden pool. Sarah's feet dragged and she looked from the corner of her eye at the ash tree whose dead and dying branches lay jaggedly against the green. Melissa was there; Sarah knew it suddenly. The pool threatened her and she felt Melissa's presence as surely as if the girl stood next to her. That same hatred which had always been with

Paul's lovely sister was here now, and it touched Sarah.

On the ledge before the cave Jack paused, his hand tightening over hers. They both looked down at the flat, smooth stone by their feet. The large drops of rain were already washing the blue and red chalk drawing away, but it still clearly showed a blue fox engulfed in red flames. Janie and Martin scrambled up the incline without seeing the drawing, and Martin's muddy boots obliterated the vestiges of chalk. Jack glanced at Sarah's pale face and then pulled her past the stone and into the cave. Neither of them mentioned what they had seen, an unspoken bond keeping them inexplicably silent.

The entrance to the cave was low, but it opened into a fairly large chamber. Sarah clung to Jack's hand as they stood inside, and she could not help glancing fearfully behind her . . . as if . . . She shook herself. Nothing was creeping behind them—nothing at all! *Take a grip on yourself, Sarah Jane Stratford!*

The storm broke at last. Peal after peal of thunder rippled over the skies, the sound muffled to their ears by the cave and the immense weight of Hob's Tor above them.

The cave smelled musty, but it was dry. There were traces of someone having been there recently, and Sarah remembered James Trefarrin's talk of the man who had been stealing his sheep. He must have used this cave. Across the entrance the endless rain slanted down, tamping noisily on the stones until they shone like polished jewels. The scent of the wet earth crept in to join the mustiness of the cave, soon smothering it altogether. Sarah shivered and Jack put his arm around her, pulling her down to sit beside him. Martin and Janie were huddled together, and all four were silent and subdued. The afternoon's ride on the moor had somehow gone very wrong, and no one was enjoying the outing. Outside, unheard from the cave, the whispering rocks hissed and menaced, the eery sound hanging in the stormy air like an evil presence.

It was a long time before Sarah noticed the tiny fragment of cloth caught on a spiky rock. It flapped a little in the cold stream of air from the mouth of the cave. Emerald green. Brilliant and clear. She looked at it, stretching out her fingers and then stopping as she recognized it. With a gasp she sat up, pulling away from Jack's arms. Melissa's riding habit—her emerald green riding habit which had been torn! She had been here, in this cave!

She scrambled to her feet, the revulsion becoming too much for her taut nerves. She pointed at the cloth, unable to speak at first. The little piece of emerald green seemed frightening to her, like Melissa herself.

Jack stared in the direction of her pointing finger, reaching out and lifting the cloth from the rock. He said nothing, but studied it closely.

Martin too was staring at it. "That's from her riding habit, from Miss Melissa's riding habit." Janie gasped and hid her face in his shoulder.

Jack dropped the cloth as if it had become a writhing worm. Filled with blind panic, Sarah ran toward the mouth of the cave. She must be free of this place—

The greasy mud outside was treacherous and she could not hold her balance, slipping on the flat surface of the stone where the chalk drawing had been. The earth crumbled away, made unsafe by the downpour. Lightning flashed brilliantly over the moor and she gripped the huge boulders by her side to steady herself. They rocked beneath her hands as the slippery earth shifted, and in a moment an avalanche of rocks and mud was falling away down toward the valley.

Jack shouted Sarah's name as he dived forward to grab her arm, pulling her back from the edge of certain death. He stared down the side of the tor to where the rockslide crashed into the waiting arms of the Green Pool. It pierced the cloak of green and exposed the naked waters beneath. The ash tree splintered beneath the weight of the rocks, but still its determined roots held firm and it hung over the pool. He clasped Sarah's shaking body near to him as he

led her back into the safety of the cave. She hid her
face in his shoulder, holding him tightly and whispering his name over and over again.

He pushed her away gently, putting his hand to her
chin and raising her face toward his. He kissed her
gently, and then more insistently and she returned the
embrace. His closeness was a comfort she needed so
very much. She opened her eyes to look at him and
a brilliant flash of lightning illuminated his face for a
moment, reflecting from the cave walls behind him.

The smile died on her lips as she saw the things on
the cold gray stone. They swung slowly in the cool air
from the entrance. The lightning was bright, striking
again and again, sending slanting electric blue lights
over the dolls. Jack turned sharply to follow her gaze
and she felt his body stiffen in her arms.

"My God, my sweet God in heaven," he murmured,
unable to take his eyes from the witch gewgaws decor-
ating the unholy place.

Martin stood still, his arm firmly around Janie, who
stared with frightened eyes at what they could all now
see, even without the aid of the lightning. Even in the
darkness of the storm light they could make out the
little images, the three hideous likenesses.

Martin held Janie tightly. "This is Mother Kendal's
place!"

Janie pointed. "Look, the one on the left. It's old
Mrs. Ransome. The doll is dressed in some cerise silk
I remember." The maid crossed herself in horror. "So
the old lady *was* witched to her death. They all said
she had been, but I'd never really thought it until now.
And look how well they're preserved, for all the world
as if they had just been made. Who are the others,
Martin?"

Sarah knew. "The one with the nail through its leg
is meant to be my father." She closed her eyes briefly
and could almost see her father with his ebony cane
and his grumblings about his knee. "The other dolls
look new because they are new, Janie. They aren't the
work of Mother Kendal."

The maid went closer and saw the amber pin on the third doll. "It's meant to be you, Miss Sarah," she breathed. "But who would do such a thing?"

Sarah looked away from the dolls. "How could she show so terrible a hatred for me, Janie?"

"You mean Miss Melissa, don't you?" said Martin heavily. "Ah, well, she knew all about such things and no mistake. But see here, there's no heart on this last doll yet. She wasn't ready to do her work on you, Miss Sarah. They're not complete until the heart is pinned on—*then* they begin to work. Like the one of your father; I reckon he must have a bad leg, eh?"

Sarah nodded.

Janie touched her arm gently. "Did she hate you on account of your cousin? The one called Edward that she was supposed to have married but for you?"

"I believe so, Janie. Indeed it *must* be so, for I know of no other reason why she should hate me. She must have hated my father because he refused to let Edward marry her." She turned into Jack's arms again, hiding her face against his shoulder.

He held her close and she noticed that he had hardly said a word since first seeing the dolls. Martin reached out and pulled the little heart off Sir Peter's image.

"Reckon your father will notice an easing of his pain from this moment on, Miss Sarah. I'll take these things with us and burn them on the church steps tonight. That's the only way I know of destroying such evil work." He ripped the three dolls down, unpinning the amber brooch and pressing it into Sarah's hand.

Jack looked through the cave entrance. "Will this storm never end?" he said at last, and the words sounded lame.

Martin smiled at him. "You're a townsman, sir. Are our country ways a bit strange to you?"

Jack smiled wryly. "There are not many witches in Hyde Park, Martin."

Janie walked to the entrance and stared out through the storm. As she turned back she saw the rough scratchings on the cave wall. "Look here. Someone has been writing on the wall with a hard stone or something. What does it say, Miss Sarah?"

But it was Jack who read the poorly formed words, crouching down in front of them and rubbing them with his fingers. "It says: *Ma bien aimée, ma vie, mon coeur, mon âme, ma parfaite—Mélisa—Le premier Février de l'an 1815. Armand St. Philippe.*"

"Which means?" asked Martin quickly on hearing the Frenchman's name.

Jack touched each word as he translated. "*Ma bien aimée*—my beloved, *ma vie*—my life, *mon coeur*—my heart, *mon âme*—my soul, *ma parfaite*—my perfection—Melissa—Armand St. Philippe."

"And the date," said Sarah, going to kneel beside him. "The first of February this year."

He nodded then. "Yes, and the date."

Martin exhaled slowly. "So he didn't die in Hob's Brook after all. He survived the accident."

Janie shuddered, creeping closer to her lover. "This is a terrible place. Whatever went on in here, do you think?"

Martin smiled. "It's better you don't know of such things, my love, much better."

Sarah was still looking at the writing. "They are strange words for a groom to write of his mistress."

Jack stood, holding out his hand to her. "But for a disciple to write of a witch? Perhaps not so strange."

"But why didn't he come back to Mannerby? That's what I can't understand. I know she was meeting him, because I saw her once."

He looked away from her. "Who knows? Well, at least he's not here now." He swept his arm to encompass the dark cave.

Janie's eyes were huge. "Oh, don't say things like that sir. Please don't!"

Martin squeezed her. 'There's nothing to harm you here now, Janie. Come, we'll sit on this ledge here close to the daylight and wait until the rain stops."

For a long time the storm continued, but then, at

last, it was over. The thunder rumbled only intermittently, becoming fainter as the clouds passed away to the north. The rain gradually slowed until all they could hear was a loud drip drip drip as everything lay drenched. The wind blustered around the rocks high above them, and the rocks muttered among themselves as if resentful of the storm's passing.

The four came out of the cave which had given them shelter, treading carefully as they climbed down to the valley where the horses still waited, tethered to the reliable gorse bush. The pool winked as the sun broke through the clouds and glanced off the rippling water. Everything was clear, like crystal, freshly washed and perfect.

With some relief they reached the grass and began to walk toward the horses. The grass squelched beneath their feet.

Sarah stared at the pool, unable to set aside her fear and violent dislike and distrust of this place, or the horror of what they had found in the cave. The green lips of the slime which had covered the pool yawned wickedly and the water moved slightly as the air touched it.

Emerald green. Sarah stopped. *Emerald green.* She closed her eyes which she thought must be playing tricks on her, but no, when she opened them again it was still there. She stared, numb and sickened. Her eyes were telling the truth when they reflected what bobbled there in the water, swaying nauseatingly to the unseen rhythm of the pool.

The emerald green cloth spread outward, ripped and frayed, but still recognizable. The fingers of a hand just pierced the surface of the pool, as if beckoning. White hair moved like fronds of fern. The boulders which Sarah had sent cascading down the hillside must have disturbed the hidden depths of the pool—and Melissa's body had made a final bid for freedom.

Martin and Janie stood silently, looking at the awful shape in the pool. Jack's face was white and it was he who turned away first, his stomach heaving.

A splintering, cracking sound split the air as the ash tree finally bowed beneath the weight of the rocks. The branches fell over the water like an immense fan, covering Melissa's body like a funeral shroud.

High above, the secret whispering of the rocks continued.

Chapter Twenty-one

*O*n the day of Melissa's funeral the weather matched the occasion. A thick white mist covered the moor and everything was chill and damp. Those who had discovered the truth about Melissa Ransome in Mother Kendal's cave said nothing except to Paul, and so the evil, unchristian girl was laid to rest finally in the quiet churchyard at Mannerby. Martin had secretly burned the dolls on the church steps, destroying any lingering power.

After the funeral the church bell continued to toll dismally and from the window of the drawing room Sarah could see through the gates to the churchyard. The gravedigger was shoveling the fresh earth into the new grave—not a poor grave this time, like Betty's, but a place in the Ransome family tomb, which was guarded by a pale marble angel with outstretched wings. The mist closed in, partly obscuring the scene, and Sarah turned from the window, putting down her gloves and looking at Paul's quiet figure.

He sat close to the fireplace where a fire burned warmly, and he stared at the smoke which curled from the logs. Everything was so cold today—such a change after the warmth and sunshine of only a few days earlier.

Sarah felt she must say something—but what? She walked across the room and put her hand on his shoulder gently. "Do not grieve for her all over again, Paul. She is at peace now."

"Aye, but the evil she raised in Mannerby will lie on my mind forever. I knew what she had been—at least, I knew some of it—but I so believed that she was reformed."

"Perhaps it was not entirely her own fault in the beginning. From birth she was in the power of Mother Kendal."

"But after the old hag died, Melissa continued her work. And the one thing which I abhor and find more repugnant than any is my mother's death."

"That was surely Mother Kendal's work—"

"And Melissa must have known of it. The doll was still there, Sarah, in the cave Melissa was using for her own practices. I shall be haunted forever, wondering if my sister had a hand in my mother's death."

"You cannot blame yourself, Paul, for it was not your fault."

"Wasn't it? I was blind, Sarah. I *wanted* to believe her and so I saw what I wished to see."

"But your mother's death occurred *before* anyone began to suspect Melissa, and so I cannot see that you seek to shoulder this burden of guilt. You couldn't possibly have known; surely you see that?" She crouched down before him, her hands over his, looking intently into his eyes. It grieved her to see him so quiet and broken. "Please, Paul—"

"She suffered a lot, Sarah. All her life she was terrified of ash trees. Mother Kendal prophesied that she would die by an ash tree, and so Melissa wanted the ash tree in the courtyard removed. And I refused. I could have spared her that—"

"*She* didn't seek to spare anyone and so I don't feel sorry for her."

His eyes flickered at the hardness in her voice. He leaned his head back and closed his eyes. "But it was the tree she didn't think of, the one by the Green Pool. The prophecy came true in the end. She was so happy when she was in London—perhaps if your father had permitted her to marry your confounded cousin none of this would have begun again."

"Believe that if you will, Paul, but I think Melissa would never have left what she had been taught. She couldn't help herself. It's as well that she is gone!" There, it had been said. Sarah took her hands away from his, knowing that her harshness had appalled him.

He sat forward. "Sarah—?"

"I'm sorry to hurt you, Paul, but I cannot bear to see you blaming yourself and grieving for her like this. She was wicked and evil, and she would have turned her powers against you if you crossed her. I despised your sister, and nothing will make me pretend otherwise, not even on the very day she is buried. I am not so false and transparent as to seek to deceive you now."

He nodded then. "Honesty I respect, Sarah, and if this is to be the day for forthright speaking then I too will say my piece. I despise your fine Mr. Holland. I mistrust him and have little or no respect for him. But setting aside my personal feelings, I cannot understand why he tries to make you so unhappy."

"Unhappy?"

"Yes, with his protestations of love, with each gesture of gentleness he bestows upon you. Why does he not ask you to marry him? You are both free agents, and yet he doesn't ask you that final question which would make you beyond a doubt the happiest of women."

She flushed quickly, for what he said was true. "Perhaps it's because he knows my father has other plans for my future."

He laughed disbelievingly. "Jack Holland wouldn't pause to consider so small a thing. No, he won't ask you because he can't be sure you'll inherit anything yet. That's why he hasn't sought your hand, and you, my poor Sarah, must face the fact."

Tears filled her eyes and she blinked them away. "Please don't let's quarrel, Paul, for I could not bear it."

"I'm not quarreling. I just want you to see clearly."

"I do." She looked at him then. "I do see, Paul."

He touched her cheek gently and then dropped his hand as if embarrassed. "No more harsh truths, eh? Except for the one which I must endure shortly when your father's plans for Mannerby are set finally in motion. Your father is determined to have me out, isn't he? The male members of your family are a certain curse upon me, Sarah."

"What do you mean? I know of my father, but Edward too?"

"Yes. I have a very deep score to settle with cousin Edward."

"But why? His intentions toward Melissa were honorable. He wanted to marry her."

"Sarah, I'm afraid that Edward was not with Wellington's army after all. Holland found out that he was dishonorably discharged and has been here in England the whole time. I now believe that he came here, to Dartmoor, to carry on his clandestine affair with Melissa. They kept it all so secret because they knew that the merest hint of it reaching your father would mean Edward losing his inheritance entirely. At least he could still support my sister in a fine fashion if he married you, for the Stratford wealth would more than cover any of their extravagances."

She sat down in a chair, her hands shaking. "Can you prove that Edward was here?"

"No, but I shall not give up searching for evidence. I will crush your foul cousin if I can."

She stared at him, at the brown eyes which revealed the depths of his fury and despair, and at the clenched fists which were so tight that his knuckles were white. "Oh Paul, how can you even bear me near you?" she whispered.

He reached over to take her hands then, concerned by her words. "Whyever do you say that?" He searched her pale face.

"Because of my family, because of what they've done to you."

Still holding her hands, he crouched down in front

of her, smiling. "My foolish Sarah, please never believe that I resent you. You have been a pillar of strength to me, a friend whose counsel and company I've come to rely on. Your family is not you—you stand apart."

She gripped his hands, glad to see the warmth in his face. "I'm so happy to hear you say that, Paul, for I want there to be friendship between us."

"As do I, and my regard for you is such that I cannot bear to see you waste yourself on Jack Holland."

"Paul! Don't."

He squeezed her fingers until they hurt, unable to stop himself from pursuing the matter yet again. "Jack Holland would willingly marry Stratford's heiress, but until you are in that enviable position, he will not even entertain the matter. He'll make you his mistress, and you don't deserve such treatment. Prinny's close friend and confidant needs a wealthy wife in order to maintain his position at court, Sarah, and you may be certain that all the time he courts you, he is searching for a suitable wife elsewhere." He spoke so vehemently that he did not know how much he was hurting her.

"Don't say that, please don't." Tears sprang to her eyes again, for she had already guessed that what he said was true. Jack loved her, she knew that, but he would not marry her.

Paul released her, seeing how he had crushed her hand. "Forgive me, Sarah." He went to pour himself some cognac.

She rubbed her sore fingers, blinking back the tears. "He does love me, Paul."

"Oh, I don't doubt it. I can see it in the way he looks at you. All I'm saying is that even if he does worship you, he will still not marry you. Damn it, he can't afford a foolish marriage. His only hope would be to persuade your father of how much his cause would be furthered by cutting out Edward and settling all on you. That may be his intention; I wouldn't presume to guess what goes on in Holland's head."

She wiped her eyes with her handkerchief. "Oh, how I wish we *could* prove that Edward had come here, for then there'd surely be no need to persuade my father to disinherit him."

"Yes, that's true—and your father would then need little persuasion to agree to a marriage between you and the great, influential Jack Holland. The Stratford name would be made, once and for all."

She twisted her handkerchief in her hands, thinking. Suddenly she looked up, watching as Paul swirled the cognac in his glass. "But, Paul, we must be addled! James Trefarrin! He saw Melissa and Edward together, at the Blue Fox. He can identify Edward."

He stopped swirling the glass and his eyes shone. "Of course. What fools we are! Well, the matter will be easy to arrange, for James comes here to dine tomorrow night. I can easily persuade him to come with me to Rook House."

Jack's voice came suddenly from the doorway. "And who is to accompany you to Rook House?"

Sarah smiled. "Oh Jack, we have a plan—"

Paul interrupted quickly. "Holland, come and sample this cognac. It's one of the finest you'll taste this side of the Channel. Even Prinny will not have a sweeter nectar at Carlton House." He glanced sharply at Sarah and she was aware of the obvious and deliberate change of subject. But why?

Jack took a fresh glass and then came to stand by the fire. "Thank you, I will. Ransome, I had a mind to spare you any onerous tasks with the stud today. I thought I'd lead the string out for you." He looked through the window toward Hob's Tor, but it was hidden in the mist.

Paul looked at him in surprise. "That's uncommon thoughtful of you, Holland."

"Please don't look so staggered, Ransome, or I swear you'll embarrass me. I do have some finer feelings, believe me, and horses need to be exercised whatever happens in the lives of their owners."

Paul indicated the mist. "I doubt that the visibility is good enough yet. There are countless rabbit holes waiting for the unwary."

"Nonetheless, I would attempt the task."

"As Sir Peter's agent you are undoubtedly at liberty to decide as you wish."

Jack smiled thinly at him and then glanced at Sarah, his gray eyes sweeping warmly over her. She felt the quickening of her pulse. He had no need to speak; just a glance said everything. Her doubts evaporated. She was his and he would never let her go.

Murmuring his approval of the cognac, Jack put down his glass. "I'll take myself to the task then, Ransome. Oh, by the way, is that Edward Stratford's mount in the end stall?"

"Stratford's?" asked Paul carefully.

"The red horse. Well, if it isn't Edward's, it's uncommon like it."

"Yes, it is very like Stratford's nag, I'll grant you," said Paul, glancing at Sarah who remained silent. She lowered her eyes unhappily. Why was Paul being so secretive with Jack?

Jack looked from one to the other and then grinned. "Well, whoever the beast belongs to, what the eye doesn't see, and so on. I have a notion to ride it."

"By all means, Holland. Take your pick."

Jack inclined his head, smiled again at Sarah and then was gone.

Immediately she turned to Paul. "Why all the secrecy? Why shouldn't he know what we suspect and what we plan?"

He looked uncomfortable. "I just think the fewer who know, the better."

"But Jack would not give us away. Why should he? After all, it's in his interest to—"

"Sarah! Humor me in this. Who can say how Holland will react? He may tell your father, thinking to have Edward disinherited, and he would probably succeed . . . in the end. But *I* want Edward's neck, Sarah, and I mean to have it. So please don't tell Holland."

"Paul, I don't like the sound of this. Promise me that you won't do anything rash if you prove that Edward was here." The light in Paul's eyes revealed a side to him that she had never seen before, a side which was capable of a fearful revenge.

There was a knock on the door and Marks came in, a letter in his hand. "Excuse me, sir, but another letter of condolence has arrived." He held out the black-edged envelope.

Paul took it, glancing coldly at the rook crest which was emblazoned on it. Sarah recognized her cousin's writing and she swallowed. Marks closed the door and Paul threw the letter on the fire, unread. "He has a gall, writing to me like that!"

He went to pour himself another glass of cognac and Sarah watched him, then noticed the silver platter on the sideboard containing all the other letters which had arrived within the last day or so.

"Paul, is it usual for letters to be sent so late? I mean, it seems strange to me that no one wrote when Melissa first disappeared. I know that it was not certain that she was dead, but even so they could have written to express their concern. It seems so unmannerly."

He sighed, glancing at the huge pile of the black-edged envelopes. "No one knew until recently. I kept the matter to myself."

"But it was in the papers. That's why I asked."

He shook his head, running his fingers through his hair. "No, it was not in the papers, Sarah. I made certain of that. I made the matter public only when Melissa's body was found."

She stared at him.

Chapter Twenty-two

Sarah left the dining room and stood in the main doorway of the house. The mist had closed in and now she could only just see beyond the iron gates. Sounds carried a great distance through the white fog and the air seemed alive with unseen things. The gravedigger walked past the gateway, his shovel over his shoulder, the newly disturbed earth still clinging to it. She shivered.

Had Jack already gone to the stables? She could hear the horses in the yard and the sound of voices and so she began to walk in that direction. Wellington was sitting in the door of the gatehouse and he jumped up, tail wagging joyously. With a little bark of welcome, he set off behind her.

In the stableyard the men were lighting lanterns, for the mist was dulling the daylight. The lights flickered in the thickening vapor.

"We cannot ride out now, sir. We can barely see our hands in front of us."

Jack was standing by the chestnut horse. "You're right. We'll have to forgo riding today." He glanced regretfully toward Hob's Tor again and then patted the neck of the stallion as it nuzzled his hand gently.

Wellington dashed delightedly into the yard, a place normally out of bounds to him but today miraculously open. He bounced around yapping, and wagging his stumpy little tail.

The chestnut horse threw its head back immediately, its eyes rolling anxiously as it watched the tiny black-and-white shape of the dog. Its hooves clattered on the cobbles and its tail lashed nervously. Jack steadied it, patting the trembling shoulder. His voice was low and persuasive. "There, boy, there. . . . Quiet now, that's it . . . that's it . . ." The chestnut ears twitched to and fro, listening to the calm, gentle voice.

Sarah scooped the mischievous Wellington into her arms. "You shouldn't be in here, you little rascal." She shook him as if in anger, but he licked her hand and wagged his tail, whining with excitement.

Jack stared at the dog. "I thought that beast was dead."

"Wellington? No. Whatever made you think that? His mother is dead. . . ."

"Ah, that must be it. He's very like his mother, isn't he, and that's why the horse is frightened?"

"Yes, they're like two peas in a pod." She scratched the puppy's ears affectionately. "How did you know that? Kitty was dead long before you came to Mannerby."

He smiled, reaching over to tickle Wellington, who squirmed with delight. "Martin told me."

"Then you've succeeded where we have failed, for Martin will not speak of Kitty to anyone, not even Janie." She remembered then what she had come to see him about. "Jack, are you sure that you read about Melissa's death in the papers?"

"Why do you ask?" He pursed his lips, smiling.

"Well, it's just that Paul says the news wasn't made public until her body was discovered, and I just wondered . . ."

He was smiling broadly now. "This just goes to show that it doesn't do to be inquisitive and unmannerly. I read about Melissa's death, yes, but not in the papers. I was at Rook House, waiting for your father in his study, and could not help noticing the letter on his desk. It was open and I caught sight of the word 'Mannerby.' Knowing that you were at Mannerby, I was rude enough to read the letter, an exceedingly boorish thing to do. It was from Edward and it informed your father that Melissa was dead. I think perhaps your cousin had the same thought as you, that with Melissa dead there was no need for him to marry you."

Edward had written such a letter? Sarah's mind was spinning, for this news seemed to confirm Paul's suspicions about her cousin. "Paul must be right then," she said, stroking Wellington and staring down at his black-and-white head.

"About what?" Jack handed the reins of the stallion to the head groom, who led it away.

It was too late. She had blurted it out and had let Paul down. Still, she could not see that any harm had been done. "Paul is certain that Edward was the one who was meeting Melissa on the moor, and that he was therefore the man who killed her. You told him that Edward hadn't been with the army when he should have been, and now you say that this looks like his horse and that he wrote about Melissa's death when he couldn't possibly have known about it unless he'd been here. Anyway, with luck James Trefarrin will be able to identify Edward, for he saw him with Melissa. Paul is going to put the matter to James when he comes to dine tomorrow."

"Well, well, it would certainly appear that our foolish Edward has been more foolish than usual, would it not? And Trefarrin is coming here, is he?"

"Yes, he and Paul are old friends. I believe they once went poaching together as children." She smiled.

Jack raised an eyebrow. "Paul Ransome guilty of so heinous a crime?"

"It was only a boyish prank."

"Well, I shall be spared the reunion of these two boyhood pranksters, for I must go to Plymouth immediately the mist lifts."

"Plymouth?"

He took a letter from his pocket. "This was delivered yesterday. It had been delayed by the weather."

"What is it?"

"The French horses have already arrived. If the letter had reached me in time then I would have been there to meet them, but as it is I am still here in Mannerby." He glanced at Hob's Tor again, and for a fleeting moment Sarah thought she saw anxiety in his gray eyes.

"Does Paul know?"

"No. Under the circumstances of Melissa's funeral and so on I thought not to tell him—the fellow is miserable enough already without this—but now I shall tell him he is spared my presence for a while." He glanced around the deserted yard and then took the disappointed Wellington from Sarah and put him on the ground. "I do assure you, Miss Sarah Jane Stratford, that *this* is no boyish prank." He pulled her into his arms and kissed her passionately. "I pray God that Trefarrin can identify the obnoxious Edward, for then there would be no obstacle to our marriage, would there?"

Her eyes shone.

Something disturbed her sleep. She sat up in the bed, her head still drowsy. What had woken her? Nothing could be heard now; the night was calm and still. She pummeled her flattened pillow crossly and lay back, closing her eyes, thinking of Jack and looking forward to his return from Plymouth in two or three days.

There it was again! She sat up as she heard a creaking sound. It was a door or a gate, somewhere outside the house. She pulled aside the velvet curtains of the bed and went to the window.

The mist had gone and a full moon shone with a silvery softness over the moor. The light was so bright that she could clearly see Hob's Tor and the whispering rocks. There was an unearthly look to that gray scene, as if she were looking at it in her dreams. A light shone in the gatehouse, a tiny speck of warmth in the gloom. The ash tree rustled its leaves and she heard the beginnings of the scraping, scratching sound as it touched the windowpane. "I'm still here," the scratching seemed to say. "I'm still here. Don't forget me." She opened the window, breathing in the heavy scent of the lilac blossoms. The ash shook its leaves as if jealous. She raised an eyebrow at her own gullible thoughts. She was as foolish as . . . as Melissa to give such human powers to a mere tree.

The night was quiet; there were no more strange noises to disturb the calm. An owl screeched across the wide moor and she glanced in the direction of the sound, jumping at the loudness of the call. Her heart seemed to shudder to a halt as she saw him. The chestnut horse was moving up the slope toward the high moor. As she looked, the man reined in, his face in dark shadow. He stared directly at her before turning his mount and kicking his heels.

She screamed then, her shaking hands pressed against her mouth. The door of the gatehouse was instantly flung open and Martin rushed out. Behind her the door of her room was opened and Janie hurried in, followed by Paul. Janie's mobcap was pulled ridiculously over her tousled hair and she was carrying a candle, although there was no need in the strong moonlight.

Paul was tying his dressing gown around his waist as he strode across the room toward her. Mutely, Sarah pointed out of the window, but when Paul looked there was nothing there. Horse and rider had vanished.

"What is it, Sarah? What did you see?" He took her by the shoulders and shook her very gently.

"He was there again. It was Edward. I saw him." Her voice was almost inaudible for her hands were still pressed to her lips.

He tugged her hands away, smiling. "You were dreaming, Sarah. That's all."

"No!" She pulled away from him and looked pleadingly at Janie. "I did see him. I swear I did. He was on that chestnut horse again."

Janie put down the candle, pushing her hair out of sight beneath her mobcap. "But, Miss Sarah, the horse is in the stables here. You must have been dreaming. It's probably because of the funeral and all."

Sarah's face took on a stubborn look and Paul smiled. "Very well, we shall prove that it was a dream. Put on your robe and we'll take a look in the stables. Do you promise to go back to your bed then, when we prove the whole thing was a nightmare?"

She picked up her pale turquoise robe, nodding, but convinced that she and not he would be proved right.

He put his arm around her shoulder as they walked down the stairs and out into the courtyard. Marks hurried down the stairs behind them, rubbing his eyes and scratching his head. What was going on now?

They walked swiftly to the stableyard and Paul shot back the bolts on the building that housed the horses. They went to the end stall, but as the door creaked open it was plain that the stall was empty. The horse had gone.

Martin came running up then. "I know what Miss Stratford saw, sir. That murdering hound is back. I saw him on the same horse."

Paul thumped his fists against the wooden stall. "I'll have your miserable neck this time, Stratford. Damn your eyes."

Chapter Twenty-three

"Saddle two horses, Martin. We'll follow him! He shouldn't be too hard to follow on a night like this." Paul turned and ran back toward the house, leaving Martin to open two stalls and bring out the first horse. Sarah went to help him, but her fingers trembled so much that Martin eventually pushed her aside.

"I'll finish it, miss. You'd best go back inside, for it's cold out here."

The head groom's sleep had been disturbed by all the noise, and he came down the ladder from his little room in the loft above the stable, yawning and scowling, thinking that some of the lads were drunk. His eyes widened in surprise when he saw Sarah. "Oh, it's you, miss. I wondered what was happening." He caught the eye of his good friend Marks, who went eagerly to tell him all about the return of the stranger and the theft of the horse.

Paul came back, fully dressed now. He took the reins of the nearest horse and mounted quickly. The leather squeaked and the horse snorted, tossing its head excitedly. Paul steadied it as Martin mounted the other horse, and as Sarah watched he carefully pushed a pistol into his belt.

She grasped the bridle of his horse anxiously. "Paul, don't take the pistol, please!"

"When I've finished with your cousin, Sarah, he'll wish he had never been born!" He kicked his heels and the horse whirled away, tearing the reins from Sarah's fingers.

"Paul!" She called his name after him, but the sound was drowned by the noise of the hoofbeats. She leaned weakly against the wooden stall where until so recently Edward's horse had been housed. Paul's rage and hatred would lead him to commit—to—"Oh, what can we do?" she whispered.

The maid put her arms around her mistress's shoulders. "Nothing, miss, nothing at all. And don't worry so. Mr. Ransome will come to no harm."

Sarah stared away beyond the stables toward the two fast-moving shadows of Paul and Martin as they rode up the incline of the moor. "That's not what worries me so, Janie. It's what he might do."

Janie led her back into the house where the long night's wait began. Sarah sat by the window of the drawing room, watching the dawn approach, her hands twisting again and again in her lap. She desperately wanted Paul to prove that the stranger was indeed Edward, but now she prayed that Paul would not be the one to find him. The dawn came slowly, stealing across the eastern skies and spreading from behind Mannerby in a haze of lemon and pink. Sarah watched it dully. Outside in the hallway the grandfather clock ticked the hours away and from the kitchen came the sounds of the maids and the cook beginning to prepare breakfast. *Oh, Jack, why must you be away now! Come back, for I need you so.* Sarah could have wept with the weight of her anxiety, and more than anything else in the world right now she needed Jack's calming influence, his sensible, cool presence which would set everything to rights. Blankly she stared at a column of thick black smoke which rose away over the moor and vaguely she surmised that it came from Bencombe.

"Come and eat something, Miss Sarah. It will make you feel better." Janie touched her shoulder, smiling, but her own face was pale and worried as she wondered what had kept the two men out for so very long.

Sarah went into the dining room and sat down. She still wore her dressing gown but did not care; now was not the time to bother about such pointless, foolish niceties.

Marks came in, his face beaming. "They're back, miss, both of them."

She closed her eyes with relief and stood, following Marks to the door. Paul and Martin were just riding through the gates and she saw that their faces were black and grimy, that Martin's leather jerkin was ripped and bloodstained and that Paul's hair was singed and his coat dusty and gray-black. Janie's reaction was immediate; she ran down the steps toward Martin, calling his name and weeping. Sarah stood there unable to move.

They dismounted and there was a pungent smell of smoke on the maid's crisp clothes as she wept her tears of relief. "There, there, Janie, 'tis all right now. I'm well enough."

Sarah followed Paul into the house. "What happened? Where have you been?" She touched his arm and suddenly he turned, sweeping her into his arms and holding her tightly. He said nothing but just held her. The smell of smoke was strong. Slowly she slipped her arms around his waist and returned the embrace. He seemed almost overcome by something—but what? His eyes were red-rimmed, both from the smoke and from lack of sleep, but there was something else in his eyes, a hollow look, a tired sorrow.

He put his cheek next to hers, still holding her tightly. "James is dead, Sarah, burned to death." He released her.

She stared at him. The column of black smoke she had seen. "Oh, Paul, I'm so sorry. Tell me about it."

He went into the dining room and sat by the table, pouring himself a large cup of black coffee. Sipping it he leaned back in the upright chair, closing his eyes. "When we left here Martin found the trail quickly and we followed it right up on to the high moor. Then we had to slow down for the trail became harder to follow; the ground was stony and there were fewer discernible tracks. We were to the east of Hob's Tor when we lost them altogether. For two hours or more we rode back and forth over the rubble of stones and chippings, but without success. We had almost decided to give up searching and come back to Mannerby when Martin saw the smoke. It was coming from Bencombe, we could tell, and the fire was obviously a big one. We rode as swiftly as we could, for the more hands there are to help the better it is. It was the Blue Fox, Sarah, blazing like tinder. God alone knows what happened this time, but the place was alight from cellar to attic, with no hope for anyone trapped inside. It was an inferno." He loosened his dirty cravat and poured some more sweet black coffee. "Around dawn the flames had relented sufficiently for us to begin searching. No one knew, you see, if anyone had been in the building. James and his wife had been planning to go to Plymouth and no one knew if they had gone or not. James's body was found in what was left of the parlor, by the doorway as if he had got that far and then been overcome. We could only identify what was left of him by a ring on his finger." Paul's voice choked a little and Sarah went to him. James Trefarrin had been his lifelong friend, a companion of his childhood, and he had died a lingering, painful death. She closed her eyes, remembering the crude chalk drawing of the blue fox being consumed by flames. But how could this still be Melissa's work? Her head was spinning. Could it be Edward? She slipped her hands gently into Paul's.

"What can I say?" she whispered.

He smiled, touching her dark hair softly. "It was good to come back here and find you waiting for me. You know, do you not, that I—"

She looked beyond him, startled by the sight of a large traveling carriage swaying through the open gates and into the courtyard outside. "Look." She went to the window and saw the carriage lurch to a standstill. The footmen hurriedly clambered down and opened the door, lowering the folding steps.

From inside came a tall, angular woman, dressed entirely in unrelieved black. She stared for a moment at the house and then climbed down and stood on the ground, brushing her heavy skirts. Even through the windows Sarah could hear her booming voice as she ordered the footmen hither and thither. Like an enormous black crow she swept up the steps toward the door of the house, and out of Sarah's sight.

"Who is she?"

"That is my Aunt Mathilda."

Sarah's heart fell. What a terrible woman she looked. Paul smiled and put his arm around her shoulders.

Mathilda stood suddenly in the doorway, her sharp eyes on Paul's arm. "It seems high time that I arrived here, high time indeed!"

He moved away quickly. "Aunt Mathilda, why did you not send word that you were coming?"

"Sending word to you seems to have little effect, Paul. I didn't think it necessary."

"What do you mean by that?" Paul went to her and kissed her cheek, but she moved away as if angry. He looked surprised, but did not pursue the matter. "You are too late for the funeral, you know that?" he said gently.

"I know, I know. Can't abide funerals. Never could and never will. Especially—" She drew herself together and sniffed. "Well, my nephew, what has been going on here, eh? Your letter concerning Miss Stratford told me vague outlines, but no more."

Wearily he raised his hand. "Aunt, please, not right now. I'll tell you when I've had a good rest and a wash."

"When *you've* had a good rest? I've been traveling for two days!"

"Aunt Mathilda, look at me. Do I normally spend

my time looking in such a state? Things have been happening here, far too many of them to explain now. Please bear with me for a while longer, and I'll tell you everything." He took Sarah's hand and led her forward. "Sarah, this is my Aunt Mathilda. Aunt, this is Miss Stratford."

Mathilda raised a silver lorgnette and surveyed Sarah, raising an eyebrow as she saw the smoky marks Paul had left when he embraced her. Her foot tapped with displeasure. "Paul, I don't know what it is that you do, but the women who come into contact with you seem to be sadly lacking in any sense of propriety. First Melissa, and now Miss Stratford." She lowered the lorgnette. "Very well. I see that I must wait to be told anything. Have you bothered to have rooms prepared for me?"

"Yes, Aunt. Melissa's rooms have been prepared for you."

"I will go to them now. Miss Stratford, please be so good as to come with me. It is not seemly for a young lady to be wearing only a night robe at this hour of the morning, and moreover to be alone with my nephew in such a state of undress."

"Undress!" Sarah felt a flush of anger sweep through her.

Paul touched her arm, smiling. "Go with her, Sarah. Don't bother to argue, for it is a fruitless labor with my aunt."

"What did you say, Paul?" Mathilda leaned forward but did not catch his words.

"I said that she should go with you, Aunt."

Mathilda's black skirts rustled as she swept from the room, and, with a sinking heart, Sarah followed.

Mathilda went into Sarah's rooms and stood waiting. "Now then, Miss Stratford, I can see that I have much to do. I am somewhat disturbed to find you like this. My nephew should know better. But still, no doubt all is not lost, and I can salvage something of your reputation."

"My reputation? There's nothing wrong with my reputation!" Sarah felt the anger returning. What on earth did the woman think had been going on here?

Mathilda ignored the protests. "Where is your maid?"

Janie crept into the room, having quickly changed into a clean apron after her encounter with Martin. She had met Mathilda before. "Yes, Mrs. Ransome?"

"Ah, yes—Janie, isn't it?"

"Yes, Mrs. Ransome."

"Well, Janie, your mistress must be dressed. And please, see that the gown you choose is, er, demure. I don't like these modern fashions which reveal everything and leave nothing to the imagination. My nephew's imagination was always more than active anyway."

Janie blinked and looked at Sarah, whose stormy face was a sight to see. "Yes, Mrs. Ransome."

Sarah said nothing. Mathilda obviously had it into her head that there was something going on between her and Paul, and instinct told her that Mathilda's mind, once made up, could not be easily changed.

Eventually a gown was selected, but not before Mathilda had tutted with disapproval over the array of costly creations hanging in the wardrobe. "Miss Stratford, I would wish to write to your father about your clothing. It is hardly suitable for a well-brought-up young lady. You have a father still living, I understand."

"Yes, Mrs. Ransome. Sir Peter Stratford."

"Oh, you're *that* Miss Stratford." The lorgnette was produced again and Mathilda perused her charge with fresh interest.

Paul's footsteps were heard outside the door and he knocked. Sarah opened her mouth to speak but Mathilda was first. "Come in, Paul."

"Aunt Mathilda, I just came to say that I'm going to my rooms to rest. Forgive my sad lack of manners, but unless I sleep I shall be unbearably rude to someone." His warm brown eyes rested on Sarah, taking

in the gown which his aunt had decided was "suitable." "You should rest too, Sarah, for I doubt if you
slept last night either. Oh, by the way—" He held out
a crumpled letter. "This has just arrived from Holland
by messenger. He's finished his business with the
French horses in Plymouth and will be back here
sometime tomorrow." He gave her the letter and then
closed the door again. They heard him walk heavily
along the passage toward his own rooms.

Mathilda was looking at the letter with interest, but
did not comment on it.

"Well, Miss Stratford, I too shall go to rest. You
and I will have much to do shortly before you'll be fit
to—" She did not know quite how to finish her sen-
tence and so instead went to the doorway, drawing
herself up with a deep breath. "I cannot imagine what
your father was thinking of, child, sending you down
here unattended."

"I was not without a chaperone. Melissa was here."

"Ah, yes. Melissa." Mathilda lowered her eyes and
for a moment Sarah thought she could see tears shining in them, but then Mathilda sniffed and looked at
Sarah. "I'll see you when we dine, Miss Stratford."

"Yes, Mrs. Ransome."

Chapter Twenty-four

*T*he following day Sarah took refuge from Mathilda in the kitchen garden. With a heavy volume of Shakespeare under her arm she slipped from the house and went to her favorite place beneath the poplar tree.

As she sat down she closed her eyes. She had not slept well, her dreams being disturbing, restless, and worrying. Ralph's handsome, false face had peered at her from the dark night, and she had heard Betty's terrified screams as Hob's Brook swept her away. A coffin adorned with a huge white wreath had stood in a dark, musty church, and beside it lay the battered body of Kitty. High on the moor, in a deep green pool, Melissa's hand beckoned through the long night. In her dreams Sarah had been dressed in white, a wedding gown . . . and standing by the coffin, and Kitty's black-and-white body, was her bridegroom. Edward's painted face had been smiling as he waited for her, and there was blood on his hand as he held it out toward her. With a cry Sarah had woken, her whole body damp with perspiration and her heart thundering in her breast. The dream fled with her awakening, but she knew that it hovered outside the window, waiting eagerly for the return of sleep when she would be powerless to resist.

Sarah opened the book, sighing at the fanciful thoughts of nighttime which seemed so ridiculous in the brightness of the day. From the house she could hear Mathilda's voice calling her name, and she sat further back in the shadows beneath the tree. Paul's aunt had swooped upon her new charge like some great vulture—dominating, correcting, and disciplining until all Sarah could think of was escape. Only the fact that Mathilda obviously had good intentions kept Sarah silent, and as yet respectful, but how much longer she could behave so meekly was a matter of conjecture.

After breakfast Paul had taken his aunt into his study and there had told her all about Melissa—all, that is, except the witchcraft. It was then, just before Paul had ridden to Bencombe to see if there was anything further he could do there, that Sarah had slipped out of the house and into the sanctuary of the garden. *And here I shall remain,* she thought firmly. *Anyway, Jack will be back today. . . .*

The sun was already hot. The moor was shimmering in the haze and in the purple distance Hob's Tor seemed to hover as if free of the earth. The heat was so great that the rocks on its summit looked almost liquid. The heavy leaves of the poplar tree hung limp in the still air, and in the courtyard the ash was silent. The lilac tree sent its perfume through the air to blend with the scent of the herbs in the garden. The day was sweet.

Sarah stared at the pages of the book. Her eyes did not see the words for she was thinking of her future. She must think, for she could not stand quietly by and let events overtake her. What would happen to her if she made no firm decision for herself? She sighed. She would marry Edward, that was what would happen, and knowing what she now did, she realized that such a marriage was unthinkable. Only one course was desirable and that was to be with Jack. But if she could not be with him . . . what then? For a long while she sat there, deep in thought, and then she said aloud, "I'll have to go back to Longwicke, and Squire Eldon." It was so simple. She smiled ruefully, remembering how afraid she had been of going back to her

home village, afraid of what her eventual life would
be. But now everything was different. She was no
longer so desperate to gain a portion of her father's
wealth, no longer hurt by his unfeeling behavior, and
no longer prepared to do his bidding in the matter of
her marriage. Too much had happened, and she had
grown up a lot in the past few months. She hoped
above everything else that she could marry Jack, but if
not, then Longwicke it was; Longwicke and the odious
Squire who had long lusted after her. She closed the
book with a thud, surprised at the relative ease with
which she had come to her momentous decision.

Mathilda's voice floated over the wall from the
courtyard as she asked Martin if he had seen Miss
Stratford anywhere. Sarah sat quietly where she was,
hoping that Mathilda would go searching in the opposite direction.

Carefully she put down the book on the limp, lifeless grass, and then leaned back again against the tree.
From the kitchen came the sounds of the cook's angry
quarreling with a maid, and the maid's tearful replies.
The weather was so humid that it frayed the most
even of tempers. The maid dissolved into floods of
tears and Marks's voice suddenly entered the quarrel.
He shouted at the cook, and at the maid, he com-
manded the scullery boy to do his tasks, and then he
slammed a door. Silence reigned in the kitchen. Sarah
smiled, picturing the normally quiet Marks in such a
mood that he was prepared to raise his voice.

Footsteps pattered along the path and stopped, and
then skirts rustled across the grass. "Ah, there you
are, Miss Stratford."

"Did you wish to see me, Mrs. Ransome?"

"Seeing you is what I am here for, isn't it?" Stiffly,
Mathilda sat down beside her. "Now then, what's
this?" She glanced at the book on the grass. "Shakespeare? Is that not rather heavy reading for a young
lady? A romantic novel would seem to me to be
more suitable."

"I like Shakespeare." Sarah felt stubborn and on the verge of mutiny.

Mathilda smiled unexpectedly, and the smile changed her stern face into one which was really quite charming. "Do not think that I'm trying to find fault with everything, my dear. It's just my way, I fear. I'm inclined to distrust every young girl since Melissa betrayed my confidence. It shook me so much. I had always loved and trusted my niece, and then to find out all that had been going on." She shook her head sadly.

The older woman looked at Sarah. "Paul told me this morning how she died. Foolish wench, to meet a man, alone, on the moors like that. It was surely asking for trouble—but not the loss of her silly little life. She had so much to look forward to. There were few girls to match her for beauty and she could be so charming, although Paul tells me that she was anything but charming where you were concerned, my dear. London would have been at her feet, but she threw herself away on that worthless man." Mathilda seemed puzzled. "Paul tells me he thinks the man she was meeting was a cousin of yours—Mr. Edward Stratford."

"Yes, that's what we think, and it does seem likely from all the evidence."

"I cannot understand it, for *he* is not the gentleman I'd expect to hear mentioned. I was with Melissa when she met your cousin for the first time, and I must say that he made a most unfavorable impression, both on myself and on Melissa. She said afterwards what a dreadful young man he was. I beg your pardon, Miss Stratford. He is your kin, I realize, but *really*—what an oaf he is! I can scarcely imagine he has the wit to find his way to Mannerby, let alone do all the other things you credit him with. I saw him only last week with the Duke of Annamore and his daughter, Harriet, and my opinion of him was in no way improved, for he's still a loudmouthed nincompoop. I was taken aback at seeing old Annamore with him; that old tyrant cannot normally abide the young men of today. I'll warrant your cousin kept silent about his unfortunate discharge from the Army." Mathilda looked away, thinking of her niece. "I still cannot believe that Melissa was in love with him—unless her interest was purely in his wealth, which God forgive me for saying as she is dead, poor mite, and cannot defend herself." Sniffing a little, Mathilda wiped a tear from her eye; she had been very fond of her niece, and deeply hurt by what she had done.

Sarah sat quietly, thinking that indeed it did seem ridiculous when one thought closely about Edward. Nevertheless, he *had* come to Mannerby, he *had* been meeting Melissa, and seemingly he *had* killed her.

Mathilda patted her hand in a friendly way. "Now, my dear, I feel that we understand each other a little better. At least I hope we do. There is much to do, for now that I know exactly who you are I realize that my duties toward you are more extensive that I at first thought. With your, er, background, and the position you'll be expected to occupy in Society, you will be under close scrutiny from many directions. Each and every person who looks at you will be waiting and watching for you to make a slip. . . . I would like to help you all I can, so that we can thwart those unkind souls who'll be only too delighted to see you flounder."

Sarah nodded, remembering that just that type of unkind soul had flourished in her father's house party at Rook House. "My father has already engaged someone to see to my education in that field, Mrs. Ransome."

"But we can make a start, for I understand you don't know yet when you will be going back to Rook House."

"That is right. My father hasn't been in touch with me at all." Sarah looked away, not because she was hurt but because she did not wish to see the look of pity in Mathilda's eyes.

"Come inside with me, my dear, and we'll make a beginning of your education." Mathilda stood.

As they walked across the grass toward the courtyard, Mathilda spoke again. "I understand there is another guest here."

"Yes. Mr. Holland."

"Hmm. Paul tells me he's the same Mr. Holland who is so friendly with the Prince Regent."

"Yes." Sarah knew that she was blushing.

"Rather an exalted gentleman to while away his precious days down here at Mannerby! I cannot imagine that he can spare the time, unless—" Mathilda stopped and looked closely at Sarah. "Has Mr. Holland any special reason for coming here, Miss Stratford?"

Sarah's face was flaming.

Mathilda walked on. "I thought yesterday that you and my nephew were, shall we say, happy in each other's company. Now I'm not so sure that I have the story correct. Who are you in love with, Miss Stratford, my nephew or Mr. Holland?"

Sarah stopped in the shade of the ash tree. "Mrs. Ransome, I'm very much in love with Mr. Holland, very much so."

"Really?" Mathilda seemed taken aback by such intensity. "Well, I've never met or even seen this Mr. Holland, but he must indeed be a paragon to have ensnared you so completely, my dear. Poor Paul, I fear his chances are virtually nonexistent."

"Paul? Why do you say that?"

"Come now, Sarah. You surely do not expect me to think you're not aware of my nephew's feelings for you? He's in love with you, and cannot hide the fact from his old aunt."

Sarah lowered her eyes. "I'm sorry, really and truly I am, because I like Paul so very much and the last thing I would wish to do is hurt him in any way. But I love Jack Holland, and I always will."

"That last is a sweeping statement, my dear Sarah. No one can say categorically that they will never love anyone else. You'll find that that is the case too. Still, enough of all that. We have work to do. I have this morning written to your father about your wardrobe. It's just not suitable and he should forward you a further allowance to have some more presentable gowns made. A young lady should not go abroad in such flimsy garb as you at present seem to have in your wardrobe, young Sarah, and I intend to see to it that improvements are made."

"But Mrs. Ransome, my father had those gowns made. Indeed he chose the design of most of them himself."

Mathilda sniffed. "Oh. Ah well, it's done now. It will do him no harm to know that his taste is appalling."

There was the sound of horses coming up the village street and Martin hurried to open the gates. "It's Mr. Holland, miss, and the new horses from France." He swung the gates open and stepped outside to watch.

Sarah held her breath, her eyes shining. Mathilda glanced at her, raising her eyebrows. "Well, I must confess that I am agog to see this wondrous Mr. Holland. Good heavens, child, stop that foolish grinning. Whatever next!" Mathilda bridled, determined that she would instill some sense in this young girl who so obviously wore her heart on her sleeve.

A groom appeared, riding in through the gateway leading three or four horses. Sarah's eyes searched eagerly for Jack.

Then he was there. He rode bareheaded and his copper hair gleamed in the sun. He smiled at her immediately.

"Jack—" Sarah stepped toward him but Mathilda's hand restrained her.

"Don't go near that man," she hissed, her voice shaking.

Startled by the dramatic change, Sarah turned to look at her and saw the blanched skin and eyes filled with distaste as Mathilda stared hard at Jack.

With tight lips Mathilda drew herself up to her full

height. "Mr. Hobson! I worder that you have the audacity to come."

Jack had been about to dismount but he paused when he heard Mathilda, his eyes losing their warmth as he sought her black figure in the shadow of the ash tree. His glance flickered from Mathilda to Sarah and then back.

"Mrs. Ransome, I presume," he said at last, dismounting and handing the reins of his horse to Martin.

"The same. I say again that I'm astounded at your nerve, sirrah, in coming here, beneath this roof, as my nephew's guest." Mathilda still held Sarah firmly by the arm.

Jack walked slowly across the courtyard, flicking his dusty sleeve with his handkerchief. He looked the picture of elegance, even after the long ride from Plymouth, and he inclined his head politely to the bristling Mathilda. "Mrs. Ransome, I think perhaps we should go inside to discuss this. After all, it's rather public out here." He spoke softly, indicating the courtyard with its small crowd of spectators as the grooms and servants watched.

Mathilda sniffed, glancing around, and then nodded stiffly. "Sarah, stay by my side." She swept inside in an angry flurry of black silk.

Sarah stared at Jack, bewildered, and he smiled at her. "Shall we go in?" he murmured, reaching out and touching her lips gently with his fingers.

Chapter Twenty-five

Jack took up a position in front of the fireplace, looking at Mathilda, who sat stiffly in her chair, her back straight, her eyes full of outraged anger. He smiled a little. "Mrs. Ransome, I believe you have something you wish to say to me."

"Indeed I have, sir. Were I a man I would strike your face for what you've done." Mathilda's bosom was heaving with emotion.

Sarah sat down, arranging her lemon-flowered skirts with exaggerated care, her fingers moving nervously. "Please," she looked up at Jack, "will someone explain what this is all about?"

Jack met her gaze, his gray eyes a little sad, but before he could speak Mathilda sniffed disdainfully. "I doubt, my dear Sarah, if he dares—after telling you so many lies." With a snap she opened the black fan which dangled at her wrist. She flapped it to and fro before her hot face, looking at Jack with an expression of challenge.

Slowly he raised his eyebrows. "Mrs. Ransome, you seem so very certain that I am guilty of a crime."

"And so you are, sir, and so you are!" Mathilda snapped her fan again.

Sarah plucked the folds of her gown again. "Oh please! Have done with all this and explain your-selves!" she pleaded.

Mathilda sat back. "Very well, Sarah. This is the

man who ruined Melissa. She was his mistress, the foolish wench, and so ruined her chances of a fine marriage!"

Deadened, Sarah looked at Jack.

He was pale. "It is true—at least, it's true that Melissa was my mistress. That her life was ruined forever I would certainly deny."

Mathilda snorted rudely. "And what else could her life be but ruined? She was one of the loveliest girls in London and of a family good enough to attract suitors by the score. The world lay before her and instead she chose to become your harlot. I cannot understand it, for by all the saints, sirrah, you're not worth it!"

Jack inclined his head coolly. "No doubt you regard it as your sole prerogative to be insulting, madam. As to your niece's unblemished, wondrous reputation and future happiness—"

He was going to mention the witchcraft! Sarah put her hand out swiftly. "No, Jack! Not that!" She glanced at Mathilda's taut face and then back at him.

He paused, looking unhappily at Sarah, and fell silent.

Mathilda did not seem to notice the little exchange. "Sir, you're not deserving of anything other than insults. Why did you not marry her?"

"Because I had but recently lost my first wife under rather unsavory circumstances which left a certain stain that would undoubtedly have touched Melissa."

"And afterwards, when the talk had died down?"

"By then Melissa had decided that Edward Stratford's fortune offered her more than my humble self."

Mathilda looked at him, her mind busy with what he had said. Sarah stood up. "But why didn't you tell *me,* Jack? You even denied knowing her."

"She hadn't been kind to you. I thought such knowledge was preferably left unimparted."

"I would rather have heard directly from you than in this other way."

He lowered his eyes. "I didn't think you would ever hear from any source." He turned back to Mathilda. "Why did you not tell Ransome about all this?"

"I did!"

Sarah was taken aback. "And he did nothing about it?"

"That is what happened, Sarah. I had followed Melissa one day and discovered the house in Brightwell Street that she shared with 'Mr. Hobson' here. I confronted her with my discovery, and informed her that I would send her groom, the Frenchman, with a letter that very day. Her brother should be made aware of what was going on."

Jack was smiling now. "And there you have the reason for Ransome's inactivity, my dear lady. The Frenchman would never deliver a letter which would harm Melissa. He was"—he glanced at Sarah—"her most faithful and loyal servant."

"I was a foolish old woman. I should have written again and again when Paul didn't reply."

"But you didn't, Mrs. Ransome."

"No, I didn't. I thought Paul's silence denoted that he wished to hear no more on the subject and that he didn't intend doing anything. So I abided by what I thought was his decision. However"—she looked at Jack with dislike—"it does not alter the fact that your actions in coming here to Mannerby are despicable in view of all that happened."

He colored a little, his eyes bright. "You seem to think that I'm amused by all that has been stirred up by your arrival, and I do assure you that that is not the case."

He went to sit beside Sarah, taking her hands and making her look at him. "Forgive me, sweetheart, but I could not bring myself to tell you. I no longer felt anything for her; that was all long since dead by the time I met you. From that moment on I loved only you. Please believe that. Tell me that I'm forgiven." His thumbs moved slowly in her palms, caressing the hot skin calmingly.

She clasped his fingers tightly in answer, and closing

his eyes with relief he pulled her into his arms. "I have never, never meant to hurt you, for I love you too much," he whispered. "In fact I love you too much for my own good." His eyes went to the window, to where Hob's Tor shimmered in the sun.

Mathilda stood and, going to the polished sideboard, picked up the decanter of cognac. Slowly she poured herself a liberal glass. "I trust that you're telling the truth, Mr. Hobson—or should I now call you Holland?—for I've already become very fond of Sarah and should not take it kindly were you to betray her love."

Sarah watched him looking at Hob's Tor. Melissa had been his mistress—surely he must have known what she was. As if he knew her thoughts, he shook his head gently. "I didn't know everything about her, Sarah, not until that day in the cave," he whispered. She clung to his hand, wanting desperately to believe him.

Mathilda drained her glass and looked appreciatively at the decanter. "And shall you face my nephew now?" she asked.

"I shall. Besides, I have no choice, have I? I must await the farrier from Plymouth in the morning, concerning the French horses, before I can formally hand them over to Ransome. I do assure you, madam, that I shall leave directly after the matter is accomplished, for I've no desire to foist my presence upon you a moment longer than necessary. The situation is, er, delicate, is it not?"

"*Delicate?* It most certainly is, sir! I think you'd be better advised leaving immediately, before Paul returns from Bencombe."

"I'm no coward, Mrs. Ransome, and I shall face your nephew squarely enough." He squeezed Sarah's hands. "You forgive me my deception, my love?"

She smiled and nodded.

Ignoring Mathilda, he leaned forward and kissed Sarah's lips. "Then that's all that matters to me," he murmured.

Mathilda walked to the window and stared out, glancing behind her at Jack. "Well, now we shall see what you are made of, Mr. Holland, for my nephew is returning."

Chapter Twenty-six

The interview with Paul was conducted in Paul's study, and Mathilda took Sarah up to her room and made her sit there until it was all over. Sarah was convinced that Paul would at the very least strike Jack, but the conversation between the two men was polite and calm. Paul listened quietly, nodding once when Jack finished speaking.

"Very well, Holland. I accept what you say, but you must understand that even if you are here on Stratford's business, I can no longer tolerate your presence."

"There's the matter of the report on the new horses."

"I shall expect your departure immediately after the man has given his opinion."

Jack inclined his head.

Paul stood and left the study, going out to the stables. He did not return to the house for the remainder of the day.

In the early evening, after a meal which was memorable for its absolute silence, Jack and Sarah went for a walk up toward the moor, with a determined Mathilda accompanying them. They sat in the shade of a silver birch tree, looking out at a tiny brook which bubbled up from the depths of the earth and trickled away down toward the distant sea. The air smelled sweetly of bracken and damp moss, and high overhead a skylark sang. The bracken swayed in the soft wind, rustling and shaking, and tall heads of foxgloves nodded to and fro in unison.

"Mrs. Ransome, I trust that I may speak freely in front of you. There are things I wish to discuss with Sarah, and as I'm leaving tomorrow they must be said now. You insisted on coming with us and so now I must ask you to respect my confidence." Jack looked at Mathilda's set face.

"Mr. Holland, I was never one to spread gossip. For Sarah's sake I'll maintain my previous unblemished record!"

He smiled at the qualification. "Then for Sarah's sake I thank you," he said softly. Mathilda's eyes flickered to his face and away again. He smiled at Sarah. "I shall go directly to Rook House tomorrow. I think there are matters to discuss with your father."

"Matters?"

"Yes. I want to marry you and he must be made aware of the fact." He spoke as if he had come to a sudden and unalterable decision.

She blushed. "But he wants me to marry Edward."

"And will you? If he insists?"

She shook her head. "Not anymore. If I cannot be with you, then I will go back to Longwicke."

He was surprised. "You would go back to that life? You would give up everything?"

"Yes. No riches are worth torment."

His eyes moved away from her face. "You are right, my dearest, dearest Sarah. No vast fortune is worth—" He smiled quickly. "But Longwicke shall not be your fate, for you shall be my wife with or without your father's consent, with or without your father's fortune."

"But your position at court, my love—I can only harm that," she whispered anxiously.

He touched her face, looking intently into her eyes. "I must have you, Sarah, and I've been a fool until this moment, striving to have everything when the only thing that really mattered was you. But we may find your father amenable to the idea. After all, he moved heaven and earth to persuade me to attend one of his dreadful house parties. I rather fancy his desire to become a leading member of Society may outweigh his desire to keep his wealth within the family. I may be doing him a severe injustice, but I don't think so, and apart from that he is already aware of my interest in you—as is everyone. Anyway, it may all be resolved when Trefarrin goes to Rook House. With God's luck he will identify Edward."

"But, of course, you don't know! James Trefarrin is dead. He died in another fire at the Blue Fox when you were away in Plymouth."

"A fire!" He went very pale suddenly, his eyes swinging immediately toward Hob's Tor. She could feel his hands shaking.

"You're thinking of the drawing in the cave?"

"What else?" he asked sharply.

"It must be Edward, for he would have known James had seen him with Melissa."

"Yes. Yes, of course."

"Unless it is Armand, although why *he* should do such a thing escapes me for the moment." She was watching Jack a little anxiously, for his reaction to the news was dramatic and alarming.

"Armand would do it. Of course he would! He was her disciple, and Trefarrin could harm her. And the drawing was by the cave where Armand had been." Jack's haunted eyes did not stir from Hob's Tor.

"Jack?" She pulled at his hands to make him look at her. "You frighten me a little."

He stared at her and then smiled, his gray eyes warm and loving. "It was the shock of having to face again that Melissa was a practicing witch and that somehow or other her wishes are still being carried out even after her death. Forgive me." He kissed her.

He picked a long blade of grass and twirled it between his fingers. "Well, we now have scant hope of placing the blame squarely on Edward. Still, I'll face your father with what has been going on here. It doesn't really matter, as you'll not marry your cousin anyway, but it could be that your father will disinherit him completely in your favor, which would be a desirable state of affairs, would it not?" He smiled at her and she forgot Paul's wishes concerning the fate of Edward Stratford. "I'll have you even if you come penniless, but I confess that I'd prefer to have you as a rich wife."

"Perhaps. I don't know. What I've never really had I'll not miss. But you have so much to lose if you marry me."

"You're worth it to me, and I curse that I didn't realize it before. But I *do* mind that Edward Stratford should have all and you nothing."

"Do as you wish, Jack. I don't mind. I only want to be with you."

He stared again across the rolling moor toward Hob's Tor, where the sky was beginning to turn to pink and gold as the sun sank. "You shall be with me, Sarah—that I swear." He looked away from the tor and back to her face. "The Prince Regent will be enchanted with you. In fact I wouldn't put it past him to flirt outrageously with you."

"Oh." The Prince Regent? Sarah had not even begun to think what marrying Jack would mean. The circles he moved in were high indeed, the highest in the land, and as his wife she too would enter those circles.

He laughed, taking her hands and pulling her to her feet. "Will you not sleep tonight for thinking of that?"

"It's just that—well, I hadn't thought about it before."

"It doesn't matter, you know, for you'll enchant them all." He kissed her on the lips and she closed her eyes.

Mathilda cleared her throat. "The evening begins to get chilly, Mr. Holland. I think it's time we returned to the house."

"Yes, Mrs. Ransome, you are right. Come, Sarah, I have much to do tonight, for I'll be gone before noon tomorrow. I must see to it that my phaeton is prepared."

They walked down the hillside and, as they passed

through the gates of the house, Jack turned and looked back toward Hob's Tor, which was ablaze with the colors of the sunset.

He took his leave of the two women and went to the stables. In the entrance hall of the house, they encountered Paul, who was just leaving the drawing room.

"Ah, there you are, Paul. I trust that we shall see a little more of you tomorrow." Mathilda untied her bonnet.

"There is no reason why not, Aunt." His brown eyes rested on Sarah coldly.

She felt a flush of embarrassment, knowing that he was hurt by her calm acceptance of everything. She lowered her gaze miserably, hating to see such an expression in his eyes. "Forgive me, Paul, but I do believe him and all he says. I don't mean to hurt you. . . ." She broke off. She could not stay at Mannerby now; it was not right or fair. But what could she do? "I'll ask Jack if I can go with him tomorrow."

Mathilda gasped. "You cannot do that, child!"

Paul sighed. "I'll not allow that, Sarah. You're my responsibility, and there's no need for such drastic action."

She did not want to do it. She did not want her life with Jack to begin so ignominiously, but she shrank from living at Mannerby any longer. She loved Jack and that placed her firmly on the wrong side of the wall; she had no right to remain.

Paul suddenly gripped her arm and practically shook her. "Think, woman! Holland is so eager to place mercenary motives on Melissa's every move, but I pray you think about *his* reasons. Are they not equally as dubious?"

Her face was hot. "I will leave tomorrow," she whispered, almost running up the stairs away from him.

Later that night she sat in her bed, a candle burning beside her and the book of Shakespeare open on her lap. Outside the window the ash tree scratched insistently in the slow breeze, and the moon shone spasmodically from behind the clouds which lay scattered across the sky. The clock on the mantelpiece ticked quietly in the silent room and she looked up from the book to see that it was two o'clock. She sighed, knowing that she would not be able to sleep. She had not seen Jack to tell him what she intended doing. Oh, this was not how it should be! She lay back against the pillow and stared out of the open window. The curtains were not drawn and stars twinkled in the velvet darkness.

Something made her get out of bed. It was peaceful outside as she looked out. She opened the window and gazed toward Hob's Tor. There was a light. A fire. Someone had lit a fire on Hob's Tor in the middle of the night!

She stared, the same feeling of loathing and fear creeping over her as she had experienced when she had ridden down in the valley below the tor. The ash tapped the window, scraping against the glass, which pressed it away from the wall. The air whispered through the branches and she thought she could hear Melissa's voice, whispering quietly in the night. She stepped back from the window, shaking, but then she shook herself. No, such notions were foolish. A human hand had lit the fire on Hob's Tor.

She left her room. She would tell Jack.

She knocked quietly on his door and waited. There was silence. He must be asleep. Again she knocked. After a while she turned the handle and went in. His room was in the oldest part of the house and the floorboards were crooked. As she crossed the room the boards creaked and the door of his wardrobe swung open. The curtains flapped idly in the breeze from the open window, moving like stealthy white ghosts. Her heart was thundering now as she drew aside the curtains around the bed. It had not been slept in.

A horse's hooves clattered on the cobbles of the stableyard below the window and she hurried to look out. A man was leading a saddled horse to the back gates, and once through them he mounted and turned the animal toward Hob's Tor where the fire still burned brightly. It was Jack—she recognized his face as the moon crept out from behind a cloud to bathe the moor with light.

Chapter Twenty-seven

*H*is solitary figure was silhouetted momentarily before he vanished over the brow of the hill and on to the moor beyond. The flames on Hob's Tor flared as someone threw fresh wood on them. She knew that she must follow him; she must find out the truth. She closed her eyes briefly at the terrible thoughts which were worrying her now, like the insistent tapping of the ash tree.

There was no time to dress properly. She put on her pale turquoise dressing gown and her shoes and went down the stairs as quietly as she could. The Buddha's head chinked as she passed and the Elizabethan lady glowered crossly. The other portraits which lined the staircase seemed to watch her passing, and the grandfather clock's face looked startled in the gloom. It was a quarter past two now and the mechanism of the clock whirred as it began to sound the quarter hour.

Outside the air was mild. The trees stirred in the slight breeze and there was a light in the gatehouse where Martin sat up late carving a love spoon for Janie. He held it out admiringly, pleased with his craftsmanship and with the thought of giving so beautiful a token to his sweetheart. He did not see the shadowy figure slipping across the courtyard toward the stables.

Sarah's shoes sounded unnaturally loud as she hurried along the path through the kitchen garden, taking the short cut to the stableyard. In the yard she paused. From the quarters at the far side came the sounds of roistering as the lads celebrated the head groom's birthday. Loud voices sang raucously as the ale was quaffed freely and no one heard or saw as she opened the door of the stalls and went inside. She had gone past the first few horses before she stopped, looking over her shoulder to see if anyone had noticed her. The singing and laughter went on and someone dropped a jar which shattered noisily and caused a great deal of drunken mirth. There would be a few sore heads in the morning, she thought absently. She fumbled with the catch on the nearest stall and the horse inside moved nervously, turning its head to stare at her.

She led it out and tethered it firmly to a post as she went to bring a saddle. Her fingers would not obey her and she fumbled awkwardly with the leathers and straps until in the end she discarded the saddle altogether. As a child she had ridden bareback and that was the way she rode the best. She led the horse out of the stables and into the yard. Clouds had obscured the moon and everything was darker. The birthday celebrations continued uninterrupted, with even more gusto as a fresh cask was broached and mugs were replenished.

The gate swung open to her touch and she led the horse outside, letting the gate go. It swung to behind her, crashing loudly against its post. She ignored it, mounting the horse and urging it away toward the high moor. Ahead the fire still glowed. It was then she realized that she had taken Melissa's horse.

In the silent house Paul awoke with a start. The gate had clattered loudly enough to disturb his sleep. He got out of his bed and went to the window, just in time to see Sarah's cloaked figure riding away on his sister's horse. He saw, too, the gyrating flames on Hob's Tor.

The track to Bencombe was plainly visible to Sarah as she rode up the hillside. The horse, after its momentary upset at being ridden in so unorthodox a way, had settled down to a steady pace. The moor stretched before her and there was no sign at all of Jack. He could have gone in any direction, but she knew that he had gone to Hob's Tor.

A screech owl gave voice immediately overhead and the horse's head came up, but Sarah urged it on, speaking to it gently. The hoofbeats became more muffled as she turned away from the track and set off across the soft turf of the moor. She had a long and dangerous ride ahead of her, but fear drove her on— fear of what she might discover, and a deeper anguish at what she knew in her heart she was about to lose forever.

The wide stream by the stone bridge gurgled quietly in the darkness as she splashed across, the water showering in droplets around her. Time lost meaning for her. She kept Melissa's horse to a good pace and all the while her eyes searched the moor ahead for any sign of Jack, but the moor was empty. With a jolt she realized that she was only about a hundred yards from the base of the tor. She reined in, the horse capering around impatiently as she stared up at the flames on the summit of the great hill. As she looked the fire was extinguished as some unseen hand tossed pails of water on the flames. The darkness closed in immediately and Sarah felt suddenly afraid. The moor was all around her, quiet and somber. The moon had vanished behind a heavy cloud and everything was still, apart from the small sounds of the breeze as it swept across the rolling land.

She moved her horse forward slowly. At first the new sound was not distinguishable from that of the wind, but as she at last reached the lip of the valley where the green-cloaked pool lay hidden, she became aware of the whispering which filled the night air. The rocks. The breeze blustered in and out of them and they whispered excitedly, as if repeating a single word over and over again. Sarah's resolve faltered with those ghostly voices, but as she hovered on the brink of flight she heard other voices, more solid and less unearthly.

"So you came, Monsieur Holland. I thought perhaps you would!" The voice with its French accent was unmistakably Armand's.

"Armand?" It was Jack.

Sarah slipped from Melissa's horse and went to stand by its head, gently stroking its velvety nose to keep it quiet. She stared down into the valley, oblivious to the chanting of the rocks high above. She could make out Jack's tall figure, still mounted, and scrambling down the side of the tor was another figure, smaller and lighter. She could plainly hear the rattling and jostling of the stones and rubble as the second man reached the bottom and walked over to where Jack waited.

"I wished to see you, Monsieur Holland."

"Was the Blue Fox your work?"

"But of course." Armand's voice was a little puzzled.

"Trefarrin couldn't have identified anyone; the night was too dark!"

"Mamselle 'Lissa thought him dangerous. She told me I must do this."

"When?"

"On the night before I left for France to purchase the horses for you, monsieur. You heard her. 'Remember your orders, Armand,' she said. 'And do it when you return.' "

"I didn't know what she meant."

"No, monsieur, I'm certain now that you did not." There was an odd note in the singsong voice.

"What else did she command you to do?"

"Nothing which need concern you, monsieur." There was a smile in the voice now.

"There must be no more of this, Armand. Not now."

"Not now? Why not now?" Armand spoke very softly and Sarah felt the menace in him. She shivered.

"Because—" Jack broke off.

"Because you killed her, monsieur?"

Sarah held her breath.

There was a silence. And then Jack laughed a little. "*I* killed her?"

"Why yes, monsieur. It had to be you. Oh, how you must have cursed the mist which delayed word reaching you from Plymouth, for you missed me then, didn't you? You could not turn me away with false messages from her, sending me back to France, to perdition, to anywhere so long as it was not back here where I would discover what you had done. But I came back. I sensed that she had gone, that my lady had been sent from me. I found her grave, monsieur, in the Christian churchyard, so holy and good a place for my poor lady. And then last evening, before sunset, I saw you kissing the little Miss Stratford, smiling at her, touching her. That was why mamselle had had to die, was it not? She was so jealous of your love, so desperate to have you at all times, but you loved another."

Jack's horse shifted and Sarah saw that his head was bowed. Then he raised it to look at the Frenchman. "I had to be free of her," he said quietly. "She was choking me, smothering me, demanding what I could no longer give."

"Ah, monsieur, with your own lips you condemn yourself. How could you have done this thing to my lady? She loved so much, so inordinately. She poisoned the wife you no longer wanted. She would even have married the foolish Edward for you, to bring you the wealth you needed when your gambling debts mounted to threaten the position you set such great store by. She would have given herself to that marriage, willingly, to aid you, but Sir Peter ended that plan. And then the little Miss Stratford seemed to offer hope of the money you had to have, and even then my mamselle agreed. She would have seen you married to another if you still loved my lady. But you killed Monsieur Jameson to defend the honor of the dark-haired miss, and my mamselle sensed that something was wrong, that the little heiress who was merely to provide the fortune was already become something more to you. You are a shallow man, monsieur, shallow and vain. You were content to allow my lady to take such terrible risks for you, to plot and scheme and even murder for you. To keep your influence at court and to keep your creditors at bay you would have agreed to anything. You cared nothing for my poor mamselle. The great and enduring passion she gave to you you took so casually. You lay with her, spoke lovingly to her, encouraged her to do what you wanted—until you began to realize exactly what she was doing out of love of you."

"I didn't know that she was a witch. I swear I knew nothing of that!"

"Oh, so that's how you seek to defend yourself. You knew, monsieur, you knew that she was no ordinary woman, that her passions, loves, and hates went beyond normal bounds. You knew enough of her past to know what she was, what she ever will be. You killed my soul and my strength." His voice was now shrill.

Jack's face was so still that he might have been made of stone. His tongue passed nervously over his lips then. "If you knew she was dead, why then did you still burn down the Blue Fox?"

Armand was surprised. "Because she had told me to, monsieur, and I always obey her orders. I did all as was planned. I took the red horse which was so like Edward's, and I saw an end to Trefarrin. I could not fail her again, not after letting Miss Stratford survive Hob's Brook—she was to have died there, monsieur. I failed too the first time I put the flame to the inn. But then I succeeded." The Frenchman's voice broke a little. "She took me back. She took back the foolish servant who failed her and who had been so afraid to return to her. She needed me still and I did all she asked of me. I came here to the cave, to be here always should she need to contact you, to do any tasks she set. I'll never fail her again."

"But she's dead, you imbecile. She's gone!"

Armand nodded. "Perhaps that is so, but her last commands to me remain. The first I have done and the fat Trefarrin is no more. There remains only you, monsieur."

"Me?" Sarah could hear the naked fear.

"Yes. She said that if you loved the dark-haired miss then you were to die for your falseness, you and the woman who stole your heart." Armand took a pistol from his jacket and leveled it at Jack. "Now I carry out her wishes, just as she intended I should."

Sarah could bear it no longer. She could not stand there and watch the Frenchman murder Jack before her eyes. She screamed Jack's name just as the moon swept from behind the cloud and bathed everything with a crystal light. Armand's hand faltered and he turned toward her. Jack saw her and in the moonlight his face was ghastly. Both men recognized Melissa's horse, and saw a woman in a turquoise gown which the moonlight turned to emerald green.

Jack gathered the reins of his horse. "Melissa?" His voice was tight in this throat.

Armand stared. "Mamselle 'Lissa? *Ma chère maîtresse?*"

The horse leapt away as Jack kicked his heels. "Leave me, Melissa, leave me!" he cried.

Sarah's knees turned to water as she sank to the ground. "Jack—" she whispered.

Armand suddenly saw the dark hair and knew who she was. The pistol swung toward her but before he could fire, another shot rang out close by and the Frenchman slumped to the earth.

Jack's horse careered wildly toward the pool, crashing into the dead, brittle branches of the ash tree and throwing him heavily. Sarah lost consciousness as a new voice spoke and strong arms caught her.

Chapter Twenty-eight

$\mathcal{E}$verything seemed so very far away. She was vaguely aware of the angry hissing of the rocks as the breeze sprung up again. What was it they were saying? She sat up slowly, her head spinning.

Paul took her hands. "Are you all right?"

"Yes. Yes, I'm all right. Jack—?"

"Will live. Martin has taken him to Bencombe." He squeezed her fingers gently. "They have a jail there. You know it's come to that, don't you?"

She nodded. "And Armand?"

"Armand is beyond mortal justice, Sarah. Jacob Mansley's parlor is his destination."

"The undertaker?" She shivered. She had watched the Frenchman die. The shivering would not stop; her teeth chattered and she felt so very, very cold.

Paul pulled her close and put his arms around her. "It's over now, my love. Everything is finished."

She closed her eyes and rested her head on his shoulder. The discovery of Jack's part in all that had happened left her drained of all energy. She felt numb and hardly able to think clearly any more.

He stroked her hair softly. "I'm sorry," he murmured.

She raised her head. "Because of him?"

"You loved him. I know that."

"But I feel nothing." She looked away in bewilderment. "I feel nothing at all, no sorrow, no hurt."

He smiled faintly. "It's the shock—"

She shook her head. "I just do not love him or feel anything for him anymore. It's as if he had never been."

Dawn was a stain of dull pearl in the east, shades of lemon and pale pink fingering across the skies. For the first time in that little valley they heard the sound of the birds beginning their morning song. The flowers of the gorse bush were brighter with each passing moment, turning from a soft primrose to a deep blaze of gold.

High above, the breeze wove in and out of the rocks, whispering a single word over and over again. She closed her eyes, holding Paul tight. "I know what they're saying. Listen—they're calling her. Can't you hear them?"

He looked up at the bright, dawn-lit rocks.

Melissa, they whispered to him. *Melissa. Melissa.*

He pulled Sarah to her feet. "Let's go from here," he said. "I've had more than enough of this place."

They went to where the horses were tethered to the gorse bush, and she turned to him. "Hold me again, Paul." She stretched her hand out toward him.

He kissed her, holding her as if he thought to lose her. "I shall not let you leave Mannerby," he murmured, kissing her again.

Mannerby. She swallowed and stepped from his arms to untie the reins of Melissa's horse. Mannerby was her father's property now, and Sir Peter Stratford would never give it up.

He saw the sadness in her face and said nothing more. They rode out of the valley toward the village, leaving Hob's Tor behind them in a blaze of fresh morning light, and gradually the sound of the whispering rocks faded until they could hear it no more.

As they reached the incline above Mannerby they heard hoofbeats behind them and turned to see Martin riding along the road from Bencombe.

He reined in, nodding at Sarah. "You are recovered now, miss?"

"Yes, thank you, Martin."

Paul leaned forward in the saddle. "Did you get Holland to the jail?"

Martin's eyes flickered. "No, sir."

"What happened?" Paul's brown eyes narrowed suspiciously.

"An accident, sir."

Sarah held her breath, her eyes wide.

Martin's expression was bland. "Strange thing that, there being *two* fatal accidents on the moor this fine morning. There was the thieving ruffian from up by Hob's Tor, shot, accidentally of course, while stealing another sheep. And then the fine gentleman from London having that nasty fall from his horse. Oh, a very nasty fall it was, Mr. Ransome. The whole of Bencombe is rattling with the tales right now."

"Martin—"

"His horse took fright, you see, sir. There was nothing I could do." Martin's mane of carrot-colored hair moved in the breeze and his eyes did not waver before Paul's close scrutiny. "Justice was done, Mr. Ransome, no more and no less. Don't ask any more for you'll get no answer."

Sarah's fingers tightened over the reins. Jack was dead. She stared at her horse's ears, expecting some great anguish to engulf her. But nothing happened. She felt nothing.

Martin smiled faintly, seeing Paul's hand reach out to enclose hers. "Looks like we can forget everything then, sir. There'll be no trial, no nastiness, no unpleasant truths raked out before curious, prying eyes. Just a poacher shot and Mr. Holland dying in a riding accident. No one need ever know all the rest. Need they?"

Paul nodded, turning his horse, and all three rode down the hill to Mannerby.

Chapter Twenty-nine

*O*n the following morning Sarah stood with Paul in the doorway of the house, watching as Martin and some of the men began to saw down the ash tree. They had said nothing of what had really happened up by Hob's Tor. Jack's yellow phaeton stood in a shed by the stableyard, and his horse was in a stall now after taking an early morning gallop with the rest of the string.

The farrier from Plymouth had been and gone, pronouncing his opinion that the French horses were fine enough, but that Mannerby stock was still the best no matter what the nobs from London might have to say on the subject.

Sarah crouched down to pat Wellington, who sat by her feet watching the sawing of the ash tree with great interest. She looked up at the shivering branches. For a while she had grieved for Jack Holland, but now she could not weep for him. It seemed so callous, so hard, and yet she could not command herself to weep, to feel a grief which was no longer there. Knowing what he really was had destroyed her dream of him. She felt she had suddenly grown up.

And yet, once before she had thought herself over her love for him, but that love had come tumbling back the moment she had seen him again. If he should walk across the courtyard toward her now— No. No, it was truly ended. She smiled as Paul took her hand.

The sound of the saw drowned the noise of the

coach coming up the village street. It was drawn by four superb grays and was painted dark red. Its brass-work sparkled brightly and on its door a crest was painted, a proud, fierce rook. The coach rumbled to a standstill in the courtyard and the coachmen in their dark blue livery jumped down to open the door and pull out the steps. Paul released Sarah's hand as soon as he saw the crest.

Sir Peter Stratford got stiffly out of the coach, brushing down his coat and straightening his red satin waistcoat. Sarah saw immediately that he carried no cane and that his knee did not seem to be paining him now. He looked pleased with life, his gooseberry eyes almost buried in the creases of his face as he beamed at her. "Ah, Sarah, my dear, there you are at last. Ransome." He nodded at Paul.

She inclined her head. "Good morning, Father." What did all this mean? Had he come to take her back? Back to marry Edward? Hardly knowing that she did so, she stepped nearer Paul.

It was then that two more people descended from the coach. The first was Edward, as ever a rainbow of clashing colors. His baggy cossacks were brick-colored and tied with mauve ribbons. His waistcoat was of indigo brocade and his jacket lime green. His cheeks were carefully rouged, as were his full lips, and each of his golden curls was set stiffly into its allotted place. His collar was so high that he could scarcely move his head, and his cravat blossomed magnificently at his throat, almost hiding the lower part of his face. He fiddled with his cravat as he turned to help the third and last occupant—a girl—from the coach. She poked him sharply.

"Leave your cwavat, Edward. Don't make such a mess of it." She spoke familiarly, and Sarah wondered who she was.

She was tall and ungainly, with a horsey face and protruding teeth. Her straight brown hair was swept back beneath her yellow bonnet and her bony figure was laced tightly into a yellow gown of dainty sprigged muslin. Her only claim to beauty was her eyes, for they were large and blue, and framed by long, curling lashes. She stepped down from the coach, her haughty expression rather unpleasant as she glanced around the courtyard and then up at the house. She obviously regarded herself as a Superior Being, and her glance was withering as it fell on Sarah. Sarah disliked her on sight, without a word having passed between them.

Paul bowed politely. "Please come inside. I'm afraid it's rather noisy out here."

Sir Peter lifted his quizzing glass and surveyed the men and the tree. "That's an ash tree, isn't it? Why all this mania for chopping down ash trees these days? Eh? First Edward, and now you."

Edward shifted uncomfortably, glancing nervously at the horsey girl. He fiddled with his cravat again and was rewarded with another prod. Sarah was instantly reminded of Lady Hermione.

Inside the house the girl sat down on the edge of a seat in the drawing room, staring around disparagingly. "It's vewy small, isn't it?"

Edward nodded inanely, arranging himself carefully near her and smiling at nothing in particular.

Sir Peter took the glass of cognac Paul offered him. "Thank you, my boy, delighted, delighted. You always did keep an excellent cellar. Where's Holland? How are the French horses?"

Paul glanced at Sarah. "The horses are very well, Sir Peter. Did you wish to see them?"

"In a while, in a while. There's much to talk of first. Where's this Mrs. Ransome who wrote to me about Sarah's wardrobe?"

"Aunt Mathilda? She has gone for a walk, I think."

"What's wrong with her, Ransome? Is she a little . . . you know . . ." Sir Peter tapped his head.

"No. As far as I'm aware, my aunt is perfectly sane." Paul looked surprised.

"Well, she rattled on in her letter about Sarah's

clothes being unsuitable for a young lady. I mean to say, those gowns were the finest London had to offer."

"My aunt does not approve of today's fashions, Sir Peter."

"After reading her letter I fully realized that, my boy." He put down his glass, beaming at the horsey girl. "But I was forgetting my manners. You haven't been introduced to Harriet, have you? This is Harriet Stratford, Edward's wife." He looked beatifically around the room, seeing Paul's surprise and Sarah's parted lips.

Edward's *wife?* Sarah gaped at the girl.

Paul recovered quickly and took Harriet's hand, raising it politely to his lips. "I'm pleased to make your acquaintance, madam."

"I am the Duke of Annamore's daughter," she said, in a tone which seemed to suggest that this was the ultimate in birthrights.

Sarah found herself smiling. So that was it; that was why her father was apparently so pleased with himself. He had managed to marry Edward into one of the oldest families in the land.

Sir Peter took a deep, satisfied breath and turned to look at Sarah. "Now. Where's Holland, eh? I've some excellent news for him . . . and for you too, Sarah, m'dear."

Paul cleared his throat. "I'm afraid, Sir Peter, that it will not be possible for you to speak to Holland— for he is dead. There was an accident yesterday." He glanced at Sarah's downcast eyes.

Sir Peter's mouth dropped and then clamped shut again. "Dead? But Sarah . . . Only yesterday—and yet you sit there looking as calm as if you felt nothing! Damn me, the fellow had intimated to me on more than one occasion that he would not be averse to marrying you! Not an outright offer, I'll admit, but enough to make me think he had an understanding of some sort with you. That's why I'm here—partly. I also want to see those French horses."

Sarah turned helplessly to Paul. What could she say now? She had no idea that Jack had ever mentioned her to her father. Her apparent lack of grief now must look odd, to say the least.

"Father, I did at one time entertain the notion of marrying Mr. Holland, but—"

"*Notion!* Is that what you call it? Damn it, he only snuffed it yesterday." Sir Peter's cold little eyes went from one face to the other. "What's been going on here? Eh? I didn't like it when I read about your sister's death, Ransome—questionable, that's what it was. And now I find you two acting strangely about Holland's death as well! What've you got to say?"

Paul poured himself a glass of cognac, offering the others a drink, too, but everyone declined. All eyes were on Paul as he slowly swirled the liquid in the large glass. "There's nothing you would really wish to know, Sir Peter, and it's most certainly best left well alone. Believe me."

"No! By all the saints you presume too much! I think that there's something going on here and I want to know about it!" Sir Peter thumped his fist down on the table.

Paul put down his glass angrily. "Very well!" he snapped. "Very well, you *shall* know, and much good may it do you!"

Sarah looked anxiously at him "Paul—"

"No, Sarah. He demands to know everything and so he shall!"

Uneasily Sir Peter sat down, beginning to wonder if perhaps he had been rather hasty. He rubbed his knee absentmindedly, and then took his hand away irritatedly as he remembered that the knee no longer hurt him. As Paul commenced the whole sorry tale, Sir Peter's face grew more and more taut. Edward's eyes boggled and Harriet's lips became a straight, tight line. At the mention of Edward's association with Melissa, she closed her eyes faintly and then opened them to glare furiously at her waxen husband.

Paul spared them nothing. He spoke openly of Melissa's activities in Mother Kendal's cave.

Sir Peter's jaw dropped. "Witch, d'you say?"

"Yes, and your knee suffered on account of it!" said Paul, staring in surprise at the other man's reaction. "But then you knew about Melissa, didn't you?"

"No! No, I did not!" snapped Sir Peter, loosening his cravat and getting up to pour himself a very large glass of cognac.

Paul looked in amazement at Sarah.

But Harriet was on her feet. "Papa will be vewy cwoss about this, vewy cwoss indeed. He does not like scandals." She looked at Sir Peter, who downed his drink in one gulp at the thought of the formidable Duke of Annamore.

"Damn it, Ransome, what were you playing at?" he demanded. "Why didn't you let me know about it? I had a right to know my family's name was being bandied about in a way which would have displeased me considerably!"

Paul smiled thinly. "I was not about to let my sister's murderer escape my clutches. I thought Edward had done it and intended proving the fact."

"Oh, I say!" spluttered Edward, crossing and uncrossing his legs agitatedly.

Sir Peter's eyes were inexpressibly cold as he looked at Paul. "Well, I hope you're pleased with yourself, Ransome. Your thirst for revenge has led to this and by God you'll pay. You'll lose Mannerby for good!" His glance slid to Harriet briefly. "I could have put an end to the speculation, for Edward was with Wellington's army."

Sarah stood, her eyes blazing with anger at the injustice of this. "Oh no, Edward was not! He was sent home in disgrace. We all know it, so don't pretend otherwise, Father!"

Her father blanched, for all to see. Clearly he had known already.

Harriet swayed in her chair. This was the first she

had heard of Edward's discharge from the army. "Oh no—not disgwace! Oh, Papa! What will he think? He would never have let me mawwy you, Edward Stwatford!" She turned her baleful glare on Sir Peter. "Do something, Sir Peter, and let's leave this dweadful place and these dweadful people!"

He was irritated. She reminded him too much of his sister-in-law Hermione. If it was not for the fact that she was Annamore's daughter . . . "Great Heavens, woman, what do you expect me to do? It's all happened now, and even *I* cannot turn back the clock!"

"There must be something!" said Harriet, wringing her hands in her lap, visions of her father floating before her eyes, and visions of having to endure the most awful scandal imaginable. "Everwyone has a pwice! Ask them theirs!"

Sarah was smiling then. "Yes, Harriet, there is a price. We were going to say nothing, but if my father intends taking Mannerby away from Paul then I'm afraid that I'm liable to become exceedingly garrulous—*exceedingly* garrulous." She smiled benignly at the whey-faced girl. She was surprised at herself, surprised that she could battle so fiercely for what she wanted. And now she knew exactly what she wanted: Paul Ransome and Mannerby.

Sir Peter stared at his daughter. He knew that she was prepared to carry out her threat; he recognized in her suddenly a small echo of himself. "Sarah, is there somewhere I may speak with you alone?"

Paul nodded toward his study. "You may use the study if you wish."

Sir Peter opened the door. "Come, Sarah, I think it's time we talked."

He closed the door behind them and looked steadily at her. "Is that your price then? Mannerby for your continuing silence on all this?"

"Yes." She went to the window and looked out. The ash tree lay across the courtyard, its branches crushed and its leaves flapping. She turned to look at her father. "What *did* you know about Melissa Ransome? What was it you sought to blackmail Paul with?"

"He told you that, did he?"

"Yes. He thought it was the witchcraft and sorcery that you had discovered, but now it seems that was not so."

He laughed. "You remember my little Liza?"

"Yes."

"And where she worked before coming to me?"

"She was Jack Holland's wife's maid."

"Exactly. My faithful little Liza is so trusting and honest. Something she knew worried her and so she told me, wanting to know what to do for the best. I advised her to say nothing more and to trust my judgment."

"What did she tell you?" Sarah's attention was complete.

"That the last person to be with Mrs. Holland before her death was none other than Melissa Ransome. Liza saw Melissa administer poison to the unfortunate lady. I wanted Mannerby. I had always wanted Mannerby, and so I sought to use what I knew in order to get it."

She looked away from him in disgust. "That you should be my father—"

"Oh, yes, I am your father. My ways may not please you, but nothing can alter the fact that my blood flows in your veins. I am sorry your delicate breeding shrinks from the truth about me!" he snapped.

She said nothing. He thoughtfully picked up a heavy metal paperweight, turning it slowly in his hands. "And so now it's you and Ransome, is it?"

"Yes."

"And your price for silence is Mannerby?"

"Yes."

"You'll not get a penny from me. I'll give nothing to help support Ransome."

"I don't want anything that is yours, Father. I don't even want to see you again. The only thing in this world I have to thank you for is that you sent me here to Mannerby."

He nodded. "Well, you can have Mannerby—and Paul Ransome."

"In that case our continued silence is assured."

"I'll tell Ransome on my way out. Good-bye, Sarah."

"Good-bye, Father." She turned her back toward him and stared out of the window. The door closed and she did not look back once.

In a short while the men dragged the ash tree aside for the great coach to depart. The leaves rustled across the cobbles in the breeze, whirling and twisting, and the twigs scraped like fingers for the last time.

Mathilda came back from her walk as the coach swept out through the gates. She put her hand to her bonnet, the black ribbons fluttering, and Wellington barked noisily, rushing after the coach excitedly until it had outpaced his short legs.

Sarah raised her eyes toward the moor, to where Hob's Tor shimmered in the sun. The rocks were so clear that she felt she could reach out and touch them.

Paul came into the study. "Sarah?"

She went to him, slipping her arms around his waist and kissing him.

He took her face in his hands. "Will you share Mannerby with me?"

"Oh yes, Paul," she whispered.

He kissed her again.